STUDIO AFFAIR

STUDIO AFFAIR

Dorothy Brenner Francis

CHIVERS
THORNDIKE

This Large Print book is published by BBC Audiobooks Ltd, Bath, England and by Thorndike Press®, Waterville, Maine, USA.

Published in 2004 in the U.K. by arrangement with the author.

Published in 2004 in the U.S. by arrangement with Maureen Moran Agency.

U.K. Hardcover ISBN 1–4056–3066–3 (Chivers Large Print)
U.S. Softcover ISBN 0–7862–6841–7 (Nightingale)

The text of this Large Print edition is unabridged.
Other aspects of the book may vary from the original edition.

Set in 16 pt. New Times Roman.

Printed in Great Britain on acid-free paper.

British Library Cataloguing in Publication Data available

Library of Congress Control Number: 2004107512

CHAPTER ONE

Sandy Stafford ignored Iowa's August heat as she paced back and forth across the dorm lobby. Her baggage towered in a mound by the door. Her sheets of music lay in a stack on a bench. But where was Aunt Lotia? She was due half an hour ago, and it was unlike her to be late. Aunt Lotia was a lady in every sense of the word, and ladies were prompt.

Dropping into a chair by the window, Sandy fingered the cool metal of the golden lyre that hung from the chain around her neck. She could hardly believe that her original sonata had won first place in the Iowa Composition Contest. The announcement had come as a total surprise, but it was true. The famous New York composer and teacher Wanda Renowsky had personally awarded Sandy the emblem at last night's banquet, which marked the end of the university summer session. It also marked the end of Sandy's college days. Because she had had to work part time to meet expenses, it had taken her six years to complete her studies.

Now Sandy tried to pass the time by reading a sonnet from a thin volume of Shakespeare that she always carried in her purse. But her mind wouldn't stay on poetry. She paced again. What could have happened to Aunt

Lotia?

Her impatience bespoke more than just an eagerness to get home. It was an eagerness to get on with life, to face the world for the first time as an independent person. Opening her purse, she felt the pages of her contract, crisp and smooth. She, Sandy Stafford, had a music instructor's job that would take her to Chicago. And she could hardly wait until the first day of school began!

A car horn sounded, snapping Sandy from her reverie. Aunt Lotia's ancient sedan stood in front of the dorm, but a stranger slid from the driver's seat, a blond young man dressed in a T-shirt and paint-spattered work pants. As he walked toward the dorm, he tilted his head and squinted his right eye as if he were trying to bring the world into better focus.

'I'm Dave Miller,' he said as Sandy opened the door for him. 'You must be Sandy. I'd recognize you anywhere from your aunt's description. Tall. Willowy. Beautiful.' Dave sighed. 'And with a stack of music three feet high!'

Sandy brushed dark bangs from her forehead and felt herself blushing.

'Aunt Lotia sometimes exaggerates. But where is she? Has something happened to her?'

'She didn't feel up to driving over here today, so I volunteered to come get you.' Dave stood with his thumbs tucked behind his belt, and his relaxed manner eased Sandy's tension.

'I've moved into your aunt's house—into the ballroom,' Dave said. 'She's giving me a reduced rental in exchange for repainting the place and helping out with the heavy chores.'

'She isn't seriously sick, is she?' Sandy forced herself to keep calm. 'No more aftereffects from her car accident?'

'I don't really know much about it.' When Dave smiled, his green eyes twinkled. 'But I don't think your aunt's seriously ill. I think that she probably just has a reluctance to face strangers with her face so . . .' His voice trailed off, and his neck and ears turned a bright pink.

'It's all right,' Sandy said. 'Don't be embarrassed. I understand. Aunt Lotia's had a hard time facing people ever since that car crash left her chin and neck so scarred. And who can blame her? The scars *are* disfiguring. As soon as I start earning some money, she's going to have cosmetic surgery. I'm going to see to it that she does. Dr. Ward is hopeful that it will be a success.'

Sandy helped Dave tote her belongings to Aunt Lotia's car, a vehicle as practical as its owner. After ten years of wear, the tan paint job looked almost new, and, as Aunt Lotia had predicted, it seldom showed the dirt.

Even with a suitcase in each hand, Dave had an easygoing air about him that induced Sandy to relax as she climbed into the car. It was good to be going home again, even though she knew it was only for a short visit. By the time Dave had turned the car onto the highway, Sandy felt completely at ease with him.

'So you're going to teach music in Chicago,' Dave remarked. 'Think you'll find that lakeshore apartment you have in mind?'

'My life seems to be an open pamphlet,' Sandy laughed, inhaling the faint scent of turpentine that traveled with Dave Miller. 'I suppose Aunt Lotia's told you all about me. She's a great talker, but she means well.'

'She's told all,' Dave said. 'She's proud of her whole family, but she's especially proud of you.'

'Suppose you tell me about you,' Sandy said. 'Why are you living in Aunt Lotia's ballroom? It's so big! And there's no furniture. I used to play up there as a kid. I used to try to imagine the parties and dances Aunt Lotia's parents held up there. But I can't imagine it as an apartment.'

'There are no partitions,' Dave said, 'but it suits me. I divide off the rooms I need with portable screens. I'm an artist, and that huge ballroom gives me space to keep and display my canvases. The light's not so great for painting, but I get by. I'm lucky to have such a place.'

'Sounds fascinating and glamorous and— Bohemian. Never thought I'd have a real-life artist starving in my garret.'

'Don't get me wrong. I may not mind sitting

4

and sleeping on the floor, but I'm not the bean-and-bread-crust type. Not at all. I spend hours on my paintings, but I'm also gainfully employed. I'm teaching art at Jeffers Junior High just as soon as school starts. My family lives out at Janesville, but I decided to move into Brunston to be closer to school.'

The miles flew past as Sandy listened to Dave's casual chatter. She felt better about going to Chicago and leaving Aunt Lotia now that she knew Dave would be in the house. He was different—perhaps all artists were a bit different—but his manner told Sandy that he was substantial and dependable.

When they entered Brunston, it seemed to Sandy that the once-familiar town had a strange quality about it. It looked as she had remembered it, yet she felt like a newcomer. Elms and maples formed a leafy archway over the paved streets, but the faces of pedestrians on the sidewalks were the faces of strangers. What had she expected? She hadn't really lived in Brunston for years.

When Dave drove the car into Aunt Lotia's driveway, Sandy jumped out and raced up to the porch and on through the front door. Ancient oaks shaded the three-story Victorian structure, and in spite of the summer heat, the hallway air felt cool to Sandy's cheeks.

'Aunt Lotia!' Sandy flung her arms around her aunt and inhaled the ever-present spicy aroma that clung to her. Then she stepped back to look at her aunt.

Lotia Stafford was elderly and silver-haired, but although she was sturdily built, she was every inch a lady. Her piercing blue eyes sometimes flashed with a fire that would dry onions on a string, but her lips curved into a gentle smile that belied the expression in her eyes. Somehow the expression in her eyes and on her lips blended into an overall look of dignity.

'Dave tells me that you aren't feeling well today,' Sandy said. 'What's the matter? And why didn't you let me know? How long has it been going on? I hope it's nothing serious.'

'Give me time to get a word in,' Aunt Lotia laughed. 'It's nothing. Really nothing. I didn't want to worry you by telling you during your final week at school. But it's nothing at all. I'm sure I'll be feeling back to normal soon.'

Dave entered the hallway loaded down with baggage.

'You help Dave tote your things upstairs,' Aunt Lotia said. 'Then we'll have sandwiches and tea in the kitchen. I've made your favorite deviled ham spread.'

Sandy dashed back to the car and grabbed an armload of music sheets, a tattered garment bag, and two shoe boxes, then hurried up the curving walnut staircase to her room.

'Nice pad,' Dave said with a grin as Sandy dumped her things onto the bed.

Sandy laughed at Dave's term for her room.

It was old-fashioned, but she had planned it that way. She had spent hours making the patchwork quilt that served as a bedspread, and braiding the two throw rugs on the floor. She had refinished the antique bed and dresser and had made the chintz curtains. Only the double-framed portraits of her parents had been a gift from Aunt Lotia. Sandy's room matched the decor of the rest of the house, and she was proud of it.

'Thanks so much for all your help, Dave,' she said. 'That's all of the heavy things. I'll bring the rest of my stuff up later. Won't you have a bite to eat with us? Aunt Lotia's sandwiches are famous throughout Brunston.'

'Thanks, but no, thanks,' Dave said. 'I don't want to impose on your aunt's hospitality. I have some painting to do before the light fades, and I know you two will have lots to talk about. I'll join you another time.'

Sandy heard Dave's steps on the bare stairs that led to the third floor, then his door closed and all was silent. She opened the door that led from her room onto the tin-roofed balcony over the first-floor solarium, and let in a flood of sunshine. At first she was tempted to begin unpacking, then she remembered Aunt Lotia waiting in the kitchen.

The impact of her footsteps on the stairs jarred the china cabinet in the dining room and made the Waterford crystal ring. Sandy eased her stride and remembered to duck her

7

head so as not to hit the beaded tassels on the antique chandelier. Aunt Lotia had inherited her home from her parents, and everything in it was precious to her. It contained everything she needed—except cash.

'Sit down and tell me about your big honor,' Aunt Lotia said as Sandy entered the kitchen. In the high-ceilinged room with its mammoth cupboards, her aunt seemed almost dwarfed as she set out her Haviland china and sterling teaspoons on the red-checked tablecloth. Aunt Lotia was always the lady, even when dining in the kitchen. She liked nice things, and she used them every day.

As her aunt poured tea, sliced lemon, and cut sandwiches into dainty triangles, Sandy told her about the contest.

'I worked hard on the sonata, but there were so many rules to remember that I really felt I had no chance of winning. I was astonished when the awards committee gave me first place. Had I known about it beforehand, I would have seen to it that you were there at the banquet to share the big moment.'

Sandy showed her aunt the golden lyre she had received in recognition of her work.

'But, Aunt Lotia, enough about me. Tell me, how have you been? Dave said—'

Aunt Lotia sighed. 'I haven't been feeling up to snuff for some time, so I went to Dr. Ward for a checkup. I'm afraid I do have a small problem, Sandy. Not that I want to worry you with it.'

'Aunt Lotia! Don't talk that way. Not after all you've done for me. Now, out with it. What's the problem?'

'It's my heart.' Aunt Lotia's voice was whispery and soft. 'I've had some chest pains off and on all summer. Dr. Ward said I had a slight heart condition of some sort. He gave me some pills to carry with me at all times, but I don't understand all his medical talk.'

'But you didn't tell me!' Sandy held her teacup suspended halfway to her mouth. '*You didn't tell me.* Surely you knew I would want to know.'

'It was nothing, really nothing. But Dr. Ward thinks I need someone here at the house. Sort of a companion and cleaning lady. We thought that maybe you could help me find a reliable housekeeper before you leave for Chicago. Of course, I have Dave Miller upstairs. He'll help out with the really heavy work.'

For a moment Sandy was speechless. Aunt Lotia had always been so independent. It was this trait that Sandy admired most, the golden thread that Sandy planned to weave into the fabric of her own life. Independence. Nothing ever got Aunt Lotia down. She had been a spinster all her life, but she had taken Sandy in as a child when her parents had been killed in a plane crash. She had supported them both

9

on her small pension, and she had even helped put Sandy through college. They had lived in genteel poverty, scrimping and saving, but never once had Aunt Lotia lost her independence.

'What about Dave?' Sandy said. 'Has he signed a lease? Can you depend on him to stay out the year?'

'He's promised,' Aunt Lotia said. 'I'm not going to hold anyone to a lease. His word's good with me.'

'Of course we'll find someone to help you,' Sandy said firmly. 'There must be lots of ladies who would enjoy earning a little money and sharing this lovely home with you. Perhaps Reverend Locker would have some suggestions. Maybe someone from the church would be available. Or the YWCA might have a list of ladies seeking such work.'

Aunt Lotia paused a long time before speaking. 'Sandy . . . I'm not asking you to give up your plans to teach in Chicago. I know you have your contract, and I know you're eager to start working. Not for a minute am I asking you to change any of your plans. But have you ever considered staying on in Brunston and working here?'

'But I have a contract to teach in Chicago.' Sandy repeated what she and her aunt already knew. 'And it's late in the teacher-hiring season. Surely the Brunston schools have hired their music teacher long ago. They wouldn't need me.'

'Of course you're right about that,' Aunt Lotia said. 'There would be no place for you in the schools. I was just thinking that you might be interested in teaching privately—private piano lessons. You could find a life for yourself here.'

Aunt Lotia paused, and Sandy tried to sort her thoughts. Find a life here! What one found was an existence. One had to *make* a life. But Sandy couldn't say that aloud.

'We could turn the solarium into a studio,' Aunt Lotia began. 'And—but no. You mustn't even think about doing such a thing. You have your new life waiting for you in Chicago. We'll find a housekeeper as Dr. Ward suggested, and we'll have her moved in here before you leave. She can use the pink room. That will put her close to my room as well as close to the bath. Don't you think that would be all right?'

Sandy and her aunt lingered over their tea until dusk. There was so much to talk about and so many plans to be made that Sandy's head was swimming when she excused herself and went to her room.

In spite of all their talk and plans, Sandy just couldn't imagine a stranger living in the same house with her aunt. Such a thing did not seem right. How could it ever work out to everyone's satisfaction?

Stretching out across her bed, Sandy stared at the ceiling until the heat seemed to stifle her. She brought a chair out to the balcony and enjoyed the early evening breeze, the scampering of squirrels, and the late-day murmur of robins and wrens as they settled down for the night.

'Mind if I join you?' Dave's voice came from overhead. 'The ballroom's like an oven tonight.'

Sandy minded. She wanted to be alone with her problem and her thoughts. But she didn't want to hurt Dave's feelings, and before she could protest, he had let himself out through a French window and dropped quietly onto the balcony.

'She told you?' Dave said. 'About her heart?'

Sandy nodded. 'You knew it all the time? Why didn't you prepare me? It was a real shock. She's always been so healthy. I can't remember her ever having a sick day.'

'She just told me about it this morning. And she swore me to secrecy. Seems she wanted to break the news to you personally.'

'I don't know quite where to look for a housekeeper.' Sandy refused to even mention her aunt's suggestion that she spend the coming season in Brunston. 'I can't imagine Aunt Lotia getting along with a stranger in the house, and besides, we just don't know anyone who is looking for that sort of work.'

'Your aunt's an independent one, all right,' Dave agreed. 'How old is she, anyway? I'm no

12

good at guessing ages, but she must be in her sixties.'

Sandy smiled at the question and at Dave's speculation.

'Aunt Lotia's age is a deep, dark secret. As far as the world is concerned, she's ageless. She never even tells when her birthday is. She says that all her friends are much younger than she and that she doesn't want them to think they are running around with an old lady. I really don't know how old she is myself.'

Dave grinned. 'Maybe she's ninety-six and just fixing herself up to look sixty. I admire her spunk.'

'Spunk,' Sandy repeated. 'That's what she's got, all right. And I hope it's hereditary. See that flower garden down there?'

'Beautiful. I can smell the roses clear up here when the wind's from the south. I've tried painting the garden several times.'

'It is beautiful, but it doesn't exist for beauty alone. Its true purpose is to hide the vegetable garden behind it. Notice how the hollyhocks and sweet-pea trellis rise high in the background?'

Dave nodded and peered over the edge of the balcony to get a better look.

'Those plantings were designed to hide the sweet corn, peas, potatoes, and green beans that fill our winter larder.' Sandy sighed. 'No one in Brunston would believe the amount of canning and freezing and preserving that Aunt

13

Lotia does in order to reduce her grocery bill.'

Dave squinted his left eye as if he were trying to bring the garden into proper perspective. 'Tell you what. Tomorrow I'll take you to Janesville. Just eight miles to where my folks live. Mom knows everyone in town, and she'll know who might be a good companion for your aunt. I have to house-paint until late afternoon, but when I'm through we can go. We'll have plenty of time to visit.'

'Your brothers and sisters are home?'

'How did you know I had brothers and sisters?'

Sandy grinned. 'You may try to live like a Bohemian artist, but a guy like you just has to be somebody's brother. It's in the rule book I studied as a child.'

'How about a stroll down to the malt shop?' Dave stood and stretched. 'After your gay college whirl, it won't seem like much, but it might take your mind off your troubles.'

'Something cool would taste good on a hot night like this,' Sandy agreed. 'I'll meet you downstairs in a few minutes. How do you get back to your room?'

'I'll go on down from here,' Dave replied. 'While painting this old place, I've learned lots of shortcuts.' With a grin, he climbed down a sturdy trellis and tiptoed through Aunt Lotia's petunia bed to the lawn, where he sat down in a redwood chair to wait.

Sandy slipped into her room quickly, trying

not to admit any of the moths that pounded against the screen in a vain attempt to reach her lighted desk lamp. She changed into another skirt and blouse, ran a comb through her dark hair, and applied fresh lipstick. For some reason she wanted to appear at her best. She liked Dave. He was easy to be with, easy to talk to. And she had always been fascinated by artists. Dave would be good company during her last few days in Brunston.

He was waiting for her in the yard, and they fell in step as they walked down the street toward the malt shop. Sandy was so intent on Dave's quiet conversation that she didn't notice the sleek convertible careening around the corner until she heard the squeal of tires and smelled burning rubber. She froze in fear, but Dave jerked her back to the safety of the curb.

'What an idiot!' Dave yelled. 'Are you all right, Sandy? That guy could have killed us both! Too bad there's never a cop around when—'

'I'm o-okay,' Sandy said. 'Just frightened. Thanks for saving me.'

To their surprise, the car stopped a few feet down the street. A tall stranger alighted and strolled toward them. He had longish tawny-colored hair and wide sideburns, and was neatly dressed in a dark sport jacket and slacks, gold striped tie, and brown polished shoes.

15

'Bart Towner,' he said, extending a business card to Dave. 'Is there any way I can help?'

Sandy could feel Dave grow tense. All his friendly casualness seemed to vanish, and she sensed that he was near the exploding point.

'Thank you, Mr. Towner,' Sandy said. 'No harm's been done.'

'Contact me at my business address if you have any complaints.' Without another word, Bart Towner walked back to his convertible, slid behind the wheel, and sped off into the night.

CHAPTER TWO

Sandy was still shaking when they reached the malt shop and sank into the privacy of a corner booth. A sweet ice-cream aroma hung in the air, and in a few moments a green-aproned waitress brought them menus.

'Do you know Bart Towner?' Sandy asked above the clang of the cash register. She didn't read the menu; her appetite had disappeared.

'I just know who he is.' Dave smiled, and when the waitress returned, he ordered two chocolate malts. 'He's a year out of graduate school—business administration— and he's managing a combination furniture and music store for his dad. You remember Towner's Mart? Bart Towner acts as if

16

he considers his job just one step above slumming.'

'He's not bad looking,' Sandy mused. 'And he has a neat car. But he seemed so—so—'

'How about "arrogant"?' Dave scowled. 'I think that word describes him fairly well. Or maybe "supercilious' is a more fitting term.'

'You're just angry because he frightened us. How do you know he's arrogant or supercilious if you're barely acquainted with him?'

'I've seen Bart Towner in action.' The waitress served their malts and wrote out the bill, then Dave continued. 'I visited his furniture store when I moved into your aunt's apartment.'

'It was totally unfurnished, I suppose.' Sandy took a large sip of her malt.

'Right. But I didn't mind. Still don't. I just went to Towner's to buy some cushions to throw on the floor to sit on. Bart's a high-pressure salesman. I could see him mentally figuring his commission on every piece of furniture he brought to my attention. He's a cold fish. I should report him for nearly running us down like that.'

'He did apologize,' Sandy reminded Dave, wondering why she felt obligated to defend Bart Towner. Perhaps the things Dave said about him were true.

'If he apologized, I didn't hear it.' Dave scowled again as he sipped his malt. 'He merely gave me his business card in his inimitable curt manner. But I suppose he can't help his manner. His dad travels a lot, and living with him and old Mrs. Winterborne would make anyone curt.'

'Mrs. Winterborne?' Sandy said. 'That name's unfamiliar to me. Who is she? I'm interested in housekeepers.'

'She's the Towners' housekeeper, all right. No chance of hiring her. And you wouldn't want her. That I know for sure. Last summer she commissioned me to do a picture for the Towner living room. By the time she finished giving me instructions, she might as well have bought herself a paint-by-number kit. The painting had about that much originality. She wanted touches of green to match the carpeting, some crimson tones for accent, and a tan background to blend with the draperies. I almost felt sorry for old Bart having to live in the same house with her.'

'What happened to his mother?' Sandy asked. 'I should know the family, but I can't seem to remember them.'

Dave shrugged. 'She died years ago. From what I hear, Bart had a rough time as a kid. His dad always shipped him out to private boarding schools.'

'Guess that's why I never heard of him before.' Sandy finished her malt and decided it was time to change the subject. She didn't want to think of Bart Towner or their near

18

accident.

'Don't say anything to Aunt Lotia about tonight, by the way,' Sandy said. 'It would only worry her.'

'I won't,' Dave promised.

'Tell me about your family, Dave. How many brothers and sisters do you have, and what do they do?'

'I have two brothers, one in seventh grade and one a high-school senior, and I have twin sisters in the ninth grade. They're all great kids. We have lots of good times together. Guess that's why I wanted to get a job that wouldn't take me too far from Janesville.'

'Some family!' Sandy smiled, but suddenly she felt sad and alone and almost envied Dave. She loved Aunt Lotia, but every now and then she felt deprived of an honest-to-goodness family of her own.

'But won't you get tired of Brunston?' Sandy asked. 'There's certainly not much to do around here.'

'It's people that count with me,' Dave said. 'Not places. You'll laugh, but I miss my brothers and sisters. I'm less than ten miles from Janesville, but I still get homesick. Our house was never really quiet, and here the eerie silence of that ballroom wakes me up in the middle of the night. I lie there waiting to hear Mom yell at Dad for coming in too late, or for the twins to talk in their sleep. And our dog snores; I even miss that.'

'I'll try to make a little noise now and then just to make you feel at home.'

Then the owner of the malt shop began lowering shades and turning out lights, so she and Dave headed for home.

The summer warmth seemed to drip from the trees, inviting them to linger outside, but when they arrived at Aunt Lotia's house, Sandy went straight in and told Dave good night as he climbed the narrow stairs to the third floor.

Sandy had never been afraid in this big old house, but Dave's presence gave her an added sense of security that she welcomed. She knew that her aunt must feel the same way.

After she had bathed and changed into her nightgown, Sandy heard her aunt calling to her. Her heart pounded. Was something wrong? Aunt Lotia usually retired early and slept soundly. Hurrying down the hallway, Sandy opened the door to her aunt's room and turned on the light. The room felt warm and stuffy in spite of the open window.

'Are you all right?' Sandy felt the cool floorboards against her bare feet as she padded to her aunt's bed. 'Is there something I can get for you?'

'Thank you, Sandy.' Aunt Lotia sat up, pulling the sheet around her as if for protection from some draft. 'I thought I heard strange voices in the hallway. Perhaps I was only waking from a dream.'

'You weren't dreaming,' Sandy said. 'You heard me saying good night to Dave. I'm sorry we disturbed you. We went out for a malt. I would have told you we were going, but I thought you were already asleep.'

'Sandy . . .' Aunt Lotia paused, and for a moment Sandy saw the familiar blue fire in her aunt's eyes. 'Do you really think you should be going out with Dave? After all, he's living here and all. It just doesn't seem proper. What will people say? You know how Grace Cantrell talks, and she doesn't miss a thing that goes on in this neighborhood. With her right next door—'

'For heaven's sake, Aunt Lotia!' Sandy laughed. 'We're not going steady. I only met Dave this afternoon and I thought he was pleasant enough. I really don't care what Grace Cantrell thinks, but if *you* disapprove . . .'

'No, no, of course not,' her aunt said quickly. 'I'll try not to manage your life. Would you bring me that pink jar from my dressing table, please?'

'This one?' Sandy held up a squatty jar and tried to read the fine print on its label.

Her aunt nodded. 'It's a new face cream. Dr. Ward didn't prescribe it for me, but one of the ladies in the Wednesday Music Club has used it and is really sold on its benefits. She said it made a scar on her arm disappear entirely after only a few weeks of use.'

21

Sandy said nothing as she watched her aunt rub the lotion into the disfiguring scars that crisscrossed her face and neck. The medicine smelled like camphor and cinnamon, and Sandy sniffed in spite of herself.

'I know you don't approve of do-it-yourself medicines,' Aunt Lotia said, 'but there's no harm in trying this cream. If this awful scar were on your face, you'd do your best to get rid of it, I'm sure.'

'I'm sure I would, too,' Sandy said, suddenly overcome with empathy. 'I don't blame you one bit for trying it. But don't you worry if it doesn't work. Just as soon as I begin teaching, I'm going to start a savings fund to help pay for your operation. In a few months you won't have to use any more salves and lotions. Dr. Ward says that specialists can work miracles with their modem methods of facial surgery.'

'I couldn't ask for a better niece. Off to bed with you, now. We've lots to do in the morning. Tomatoes are ripe, and there may be sweet corn just waiting to be picked. And there are always green beans to be canned.'

'But you're not to overdo. Remember?'

Sandy went back to her room and crawled into bed, but sleep would not come. Even with her eyes closed she could still see her aunt's frail form in the ancient bed. With a heart condition, could she stand the surgery required to mend her face? Sandy turned and squirmed, and an hour later when she was just dropping off to sleep, her aunt called again.

'Yes, Aunt Lotia?' Grabbing her robe and blinking against the sudden brightness of the hall light, Sandy poked her head into her aunt's room.

'Sandy, would you please bring me a drink? I usually leave a glass of water here on my night table, but I must have forgotten it tonight. My throat is dry, and my mouth is absolutely parched. I'm sorry to have to awaken you.'

'I'll be glad to get it for you.' Sandy hurried to the bathroom, found a glass, and filled it with water from the tap. How frail Aunt Lotia looks! she thought. Not at all like her usual self. Yet she had seemed well earlier in the evening.

'Thank you, dear,' her aunt said. 'Family means so much to a person when he gets the least bit helpless. It's hard for the weak not to impose on the strong. Now you run back to bed. I'll put the glass right here where I can reach it.'

By the time Sandy got back to her room, she was wide awake again. She stepped out on the balcony for a few moments. The scent of roses drifted to her on the south breeze, and she felt a misty dampness against her cheeks. How could Dave complain of the silence? she wondered. The night was full of sounds.

In the distance she heard frogs croaking;

close to the house crickets chirped; somewhere in the maze of oak branches a hoot owl wailed into the night. The owl's call was more sad than frightening, and Sandy's somber thoughts returned to plague her.

How could she leave Aunt Lotia now? Such a separation would have been hard enough had her aunt been in good health. But to go off to Chicago and leave her alone with her weak heart was unthinkable.

What stranger would bring her aunt medicine in the night? What hired person would hear and answer her every weak call? In that instant Sandy reached the decision that she knew she should have reached earlier at the supper table.

She felt hollow inside, like the time when she had lost the cameo pendant that had belonged to her mother. But she knew her decision was the right one. She must put Aunt Lotia's needs before her own desires. She would stay here in Brunston. The Chicago school would have no trouble finding another teacher. Sandy knew there were too many applicants for the number of jobs available.

She sighed and watched the trail of a shooting star as it streaked across the sky. As it disappeared, it seemed to symbolize the end of her own dreams. Gone was her goal of independence. Gone were her plans for a sophisticated life in a big city. Gone were her hopes for an exciting career in teaching.

It was a momentous decision, and Sandy felt a need to tell someone, but she hated to disturb her aunt's sleep. Dave had to know sooner or later. In fact, he had to know before he made any plans for his mother to help them find a suitable housekeeper. Sandy knew she was rationalizing, but she had to talk to someone, and Dave was the likely choice.

'Dave,' Sandy called softly toward the French windows. 'Dave.' No answer. Picking up a twig from the balcony floor, Sandy pitched it at Dave's window and listened as it hit against the screen, then bounced back onto the tin roof. 'Dave, are you awake?'

In a matter of seconds Dave's head appeared at the window. 'What goes down there? I had a feeling that someone was trying to send me secret signals.'

Sandy suddenly felt foolish. It wouldn't matter one way or another to Dave whether she stayed in Brunston or moved to Chicago. But she had to say what was on her mind now that Dave was at the window peering down at her.

'I know it's the middle of the night, but I thought you should know that I've decided to stay on here with Aunt Lotia this fall and winter. Your mom won't need to help us find a housekeeper.'

'For this you wake me up?' Dave sat down on the low window ledge and relaxed as if he were in a comfortable arm chair.

25

'I'm sorry,' Sandy said. 'I shouldn't have bothered you, but I had to tell someone.'

'I was only joking.' Dave dug his thumbs behind the scarred belt he wore. 'I wasn't asleep. I was at the other end of the ballroom reading. I try to read a biography of a great artist each week. The story of their lives gives me insight into my own problems.' With an easy jump he landed beside Sandy on the balcony.

'I'm scared,' she confessed. 'I'm quite a little selfish and just plain scared.'

'Of me?' Dave asked. 'I'm harmless. Really, all the stories you hear about artists aren't true.'

'I'm not scared of you, silly. I'm scared of myself, I guess. I haven't told Aunt Lotia that I'm going to stay in Brunston. But I can't go off and leave her here with a housekeeper. I'd never forgive myself if anything happened to her while I was away.'

'I admire you.' Dave squinted his left eye and stared at Sandy in that special way of his. 'I really admire you.'

'Don't admire me. I'm nothing but a coward. I just told you that I'm scared to death. I'm sitting here thinking about myself instead of about Aunt Lotia.

'Just think! All her life she has sacrificed herself for others. First her mother needed her at home to help with the younger children, so she never married. Then, after the children left home, her father was paralyzed by a stroke, so she stayed on to help her mother care for him.

'When both parents died, Aunt Lotia was left alone. Then I came along. My folks had plenty of relatives, but Aunt Lotia was the only one who volunteered to take me in.'

'She's a great person,' Dave said. 'In a way she's taken me in, too,'

'I'm afraid,' Sandy repeated. 'If I change my plans, give up my job and a life in Chicago to stay here with her, will my whole existence be one sacrifice after another? Will I end up a lonely spinster like Aunt Lotia?'

'I doubt that,' Dave answered with a smile. 'Anyway, who says she's lonely? She has lots of friends and relatives.'

Sandy hardly heard Dave's words, and when she spoke again, it was more to herself than to Dave. 'I used to think that the world was an okay place, that everything would turn out all right one way or another. But it isn't an okay place, is it? Everything isn't going to turn out all right. First my parents were killed, and now, just when I'm ready to try life on my own, Aunt Lotia gets sick. I want to be independent, but now I'll be tied down here in Brunston. It isn't fair!'

'You're really feeling sorry for yourself, aren't you?' Dave was bristling. His relaxed manner had vanished, and he stood stiff and straight. 'Did someone promise you a fair world? Did they? It's a crazy-mixed-up world, and there's nothing fair about it. But it's our duty to make a reasonable response to it instead of whining and complaining.'

'I'm sorry.' Sandy was suddenly aware of how she must sound. 'I won't whine on your shoulder ever again. It's just that I used to believe in freedom of choice. I used to think that a person could make his life according to his own desires. But now everything seems out of my hands. How can I be independent when my whole life seems predestined?'

'Maybe there's still freedom and independence within restrictions,' Dave suggested.

'What's that supposed to mean?'

'Figure it out for yourself.' Dave's voice was curt and crisp. 'I've got to get some sleep. Tomorrow's a work day.' Using the screen door for a brace, he hoisted himself back up to his own apartment. He closed his window and disappeared from view without another glance in Sandy's direction.

Sandy sat outside for so long that the night dew dampened her hair and skin. What must Dave think of her! She hadn't meant to complain, and she had thought he would understand how she felt. But why should he understand her? They had only met a few short hours ago. They knew little of each other.

Unconsciously Sandy's fingers touched the

lyre she wore around her neck. Freedom within restrictions. Dave's words re-echoed in her mind. Hadn't she won an award for that very thing? Didn't a sonata consist of melodic freedom set in a multitude of restrictions? And Shakespeare! He wrote some of his best works in sonnet form, works she loved to read and reread. And wasn't a sonnet one of the most restrictive forms of poetry? Sandy sighed. But her life was neither a sonata nor a sonnet. How was she ever going to manage?

CHAPTER THREE

The next morning Sandy rose before the sun had burned the dew from the air. The Stafford house was silent as she wrote a letter to the Chicago school, explaining why she must break her contract at the last minute.

Creeping from the house, Sandy felt the morning breeze cool her cheeks as she walked to the corner mailbox to post the message. There! The deed was done. There was no changing her mind now.

When she returned to the house, she tiptoed to the kitchen and started breakfast. Would she be performing this same chore in this same place forty years from now? The thought made her cringe inwardly. She wished she could find a rational response to this crazy world as Dave had suggested.

The fragrance of coffee filled the air before Aunt Lotia appeared in the doorway wearing the sky-blue robe that made her complexion look milky pale.

'Now, Sandy! I won't have you waiting on me as if I were an invalid. Dr. Ward said I was perfectly able to do my ordinary household chores. I'm just to avoid exertion. That's why I've hired Dave to do the heavy work.'

'I'm not treating you like an invalid.' Sandy poured their morning coffee and forced brightness into her voice. 'I just mailed a letter to Chicago, telling the school board that I won't be teaching there this fall. Since I was already up and dressed, I decided that I might as well get breakfast.'

'Sandy!' Aunt Lotia dropped onto a kitchen chair. 'You've given up your job! I had no right to suggest it. I had no right.'

The fire in Aunt Lotia's eyes died, and her mouth drooped in a strange expression that Sandy didn't recognize. It was almost a look of guilt. Sandy didn't want her aunt to feel guilty.

'I did this because I wanted to,' Sandy said. 'You must believe that. Chicago can wait. Starting a private piano studio in Brunston as you suggested will be a challenge. That's what I've decided to do. But are you sure you want to open your home to hordes of private pupils? I'm sure it will cause noise and inconvenience.'

'I won't be opening my whole home,' Aunt Lotia said, regaining her composure. 'Just the solarium. It has its own entrance, remember? And with all those velvet hangings on the walls, it is fairly soundproof. If the door to the main part of the house is closed, there should be little disturbance.'

Sandy drank her coffee and refilled her cup. She needed strength and stimulation. She had no idea of how to start a private piano studio. How would she get pupils? Did one simply place an advertisement in the paper and hope for the best? What if no one wanted to take lessons? As if reading her mind, her aunt began making plans.

'There are several piano teachers in Brunston, so you'll have stiff competition, Sandy. I think the first thing you should do is to give a recital. Let the townspeople hear what you can do. That'll bring pupils quicker than anything else I can think of.'

'Where would I give it?' Sandy asked, wondering at her aunt's enthusiasm. The old fire was back in her eyes now.

'There's a wonderful auditorium at the art center. If my Wednesday Music Club sponsors your recital, you may use the center's facilities free of charge. Of course, you may not ask an admission fee for the recital—against the rules. But a recital will introduce you to the community as a professional musician. Could you be ready in two weeks—the first of

September?'

'I'm in practice,' Sandy said. 'I've spent hours at the piano all summer long. But what about your club? Do you think they'll agree to sponsor me?'

'They'll be delighted,' Aunt Lotia said. 'Don't forget that Grace Cantrell attended your senior recital. She knows what you can do, and she's president of the club. And its purpose is to promote musical interest in the community.'

'A piano recital might do that,' Sandy said thoughtfully.

'I'll take care of all the details. You concentrate on preparing your program.' Aunt Lotia began making notes on the back of an envelope.

'I'll use the same program I used last spring for my senior recital. I still have those numbers memorized and ready for performance. And I might add my original sonata, perhaps as an encore. Do you think the audience would enjoy hearing it?'

'I'm sure they would. And the newspaper will give you some nice publicity about the award you won. I'll see to that. Excuse me a moment.' Aunt Lotia shoved her chair from the table. 'I have some telephone calls to make.'

Sandy washed their few breakfast dishes, then hurried to her room to straighten up. If a recital was in the offing, she had to set a rigid practice schedule. Three or four hours a day at the piano should strengthen her finger muscles and keep her hands in shape. She wondered if Aunt Lotia's old piano was in good condition. Perhaps she should call the tuner.

Sorting through her music, Sandy pushed out the numbers she intended to review for her performance in Brunston. She had most of them thoroughly memorized, but she would give them daily practice, along with lots of scales, chords, and finger exercises. If her future in Brunston depended on a piano recital, she knew it was up to her to give a superior performance.

As she headed for the solarium, Aunt Lotia met her in the hallway. 'It's fairly well settled, Sandy. I called Grace Cantrell. She feels sure that the club will be delighted to sponsor you. She'll take a vote of the board members by telephone this morning and let me know definitely. But she said for us to go ahead and make our plans. She's that sure of the club— and of you and your performance.'

'My, but you do work quickly.' Sandy grinned and arranged her music on the piano. She uncovered the keyboard and listened to the pitch of some octave scales.

'Does Brunston have a piano tuner?' she asked.

'Yes, but we won't need him just yet,' Aunt Lotia said. 'I also made one other call. I want you to have the best piano available for your recital and for practice. This one isn't good enough.'

'Aunt Lotia! We can't afford a new piano. I won't go into debt or let *you* go into debt for this venture. What if I can't get any pupils? How would we ever pay the money back?'

'There'll be no going into debt. I've called Towner's Mart. They'll loan you the use of one of their pianos in exchange for the advertising it will bring their store. All you have to do is to let them put up one small sign giving them credit for the piano.'

'But they've never heard of me,' Sandy protested. 'They really don't know whether or not I play well. How can they do this for a stranger?'

'Don't forget that they know me,' Aunt Lotia countered. 'And they know Grace. They've known us for years, and they know we wouldn't sponsor you unless we were sure of success.'

Sandy sighed, her thoughts in a whirl.

'How soon can you get dressed?' Aunt Lotia asked. 'Mr. Towner suggested that you come down to his store this morning and try out some pianos. If they have nothing in stock that you like, they'll place a special order and get some selections from Chicago.'

'I'll be ready in a jiffy.' Sandy's heart pounded. What had happened to the quiet Brunston life she had imagined! If this was freedom within restrictions, she liked it. 'You'll

34

go with me, won't you?' she called to her aunt over her shoulder as she hurried upstairs.

'Of course I'll go. I'll give you a personal introduction to Bart Towner. I don't believe you've ever met him, but I've known his family for years. Poor, poor boy. He's had a miserable life. But that's all past. He's doing well in his father's store.'

Bart Towner! The name brought back memories of last night's terrifying street scene. Sandy's fingers grew icy, but she couldn't bring herself to tell her aunt of her meeting with Bart. And why should she? That should remain a secret between herself and Dave. There was no point in upsetting Aunt Lotia over something that couldn't be helped. Anyway, Bart Towner might not even remember her. It had been dark, and everything had happened so fast that they all had been upset and edgy.

Sandy dressed in her brightest shift, one she had made just before summer school started. She knew it was the perfect foil for her coloring. She secured her long, straight hair in a coil on top of her head, then applied a light touch of make-up. Why was she so nervous? She wasn't going to town for a personal visit with Bart Towner. She was only going to look at some pianos.

Aunt Lotia drove them to town. Wearing a high ruffled collar that tried but failed to hide her facial scars, she sat behind the steering

35

wheel like a queen on a throne. She parked right in front of Towner's Mart, and when they entered the store, she let Sandy precede her. The store smelled of furniture polish, but Sandy forgot that as her heels sank into deep carpeting.

'May I help you?' a clerk asked.

'We've come to look at some pianos,' Sandy replied, feeling out of place and unsure of herself.

Aunt Lotia cleared her throat, and her eyes snapped. 'Young man, we have an appointment with Bart Towner. Will you please tell him that we are here? He's expecting us.'

'He's busy with another customer right now,' the clerk said. 'Please have a chair. I'll tell him you're here, and I'm sure he'll be right with you.'

Sandy marveled at her aunt's ability to manage a situation. Who would believe that she had a weak heart! She hardly seemed like the same person who had helplessly requested water and medicine during the night.

They sat down, and Sandy saw Bart Towner showing a young couple an expensive living-room suite. He tilted his head and looked at them in an appraising manner, as if merely curious to see their reaction to the furniture.

The young man frowned and tried to steer his wife to a less expensive set, but Bart kept maneuvering them back to the expensive furniture. Later Sandy saw the couple sign a paper, and she heard Bart order the expensive set of furniture delivered to their address.

Sandy was puzzled. She couldn't decide whether she disliked Bart as a high-pressure salesman or whether she admired him for his sales ability. He had a way with words, and he certainly knew how to handle people. But would he try to high-pressure Aunt Lotia into buying a piano? Sandy wouldn't stand for that. She wouldn't let her aunt go into debt for her.

Sandy needn't have worried. Aunt Lotia performed the introductions, and if Bart recognized Sandy, he didn't acknowledge it. Nor did he try any high-pressure tactics. He seemed to know that he was no match for Lotia Stafford.

'I'd like to have you try this piano.' Bart indicated a console, and as he leaned over to open it, Sandy smelled a lemony after-shave lotion.

'It's sometimes called an upright grand,' Bart explained, 'because it has the same inside structure as a small grand piano. And, of course, it has the same tone quality. Try it.' Bart pulled out the piano bench and stood back so that Sandy could seat herself.

She played part of the first movement of her sonata and was impressed with the action and tone quality of the instrument. Bart Towner was impressed with her playing. He asked her to try several other pianos.

'You really should be performing on a grand,' he said enthusiastically. 'Your talent deserves the very best.'

'But that wouldn't be fair to your store or to you,' Sandy protested. 'You need advertising. It's my guess that few people in Brunston will be buying grand pianos. But several families might purchase smaller models for their children to learn on. I'm perfectly willing to perform on a console.'

'What type of instrument are you using at home?' Bart asked.

'The spinet your father sold me years ago.' Aunt Lotia spoke before Sandy could reply. 'It's always been quite adequate for our needs up until now.'

'But your niece should be practicing on the instrument that she'll perform on,' Bart insisted. 'We'll bring this console to your home and let you use it until recital time.'

'Oh, that's too much trouble,' Sandy declared. 'The moving and all—'

'We have men and equipment to take care of that,' Bart said smoothly. 'In the long run, I'm sure it will mean much more to us than it will to you.'

'I really don't know if it will fit into the solarium.' Aunt Lotia stood back and studied the piano from all angles. 'Bart, why don't you plan to come to the house for dinner tonight? It's been ages since I've cooked for a handsome young man. You can bring a tape and take some measurements of the solarium and see what you think about moving another piano in.'

Sandy felt herself blushing. Why was Aunt Lotia putting Bart Towner on the spot like this? Of course the piano would fit into the solarium. Sandy knew that without taking any measurements. Why was Aunt Lotia making such an issue of space? Had she changed her mind about the recital? To Sandy's surprise, Bart Towner accepted the invitation.

'I'd love to have dinner with you, Miss Stafford. It would be a pleasure. What time would be convenient?'

'Come around seven o'clock,' Aunt Lotia said. 'And bring your best appetite.'

After that the rest of the day flew by. Sandy spent several hours practicing on their old piano in spite of the poor tuning. Then she helped her aunt set the table and straighten up the living room. At four in the afternoon, Aunt Lotia insisted that Dave stop painting the house. The smell was permeating the entire downstairs area.

Sandy wondered why she was so nervous. She had helped her aunt serve company dinners before. This was nothing new, and there was nothing to worry about, nothing but Bart Towner. He had seemed so different in the store from the way he had behaved the night before. Today he had been suave and sophisticated, and there had been no trace of the arrogance Dave had objected to. Sandy found herself humming. A girl could fall for a boy like Bart Towner.

By the time Bart arrived for dinner, the aroma of roast beef and gravy had replaced the paint smell that threatened the house. Again he was wearing a gold striped necktie, and he carried a bouquet of roses for Aunt Lotia, who made a big show of displaying them in a cut-glass vase that she placed on top of the walnut bookcase.

Everything about the meal went well. Bart praised Aunt Lotia's cooking until he made her blush. It wasn't until they were having their after-dinner coffee that Sandy remembered the true reason for Bart's visit.

'Do come and see the solarium,' she offered. 'It's a bit crowded, but perhaps some of the furniture could be rearranged, or removed from the room entirely. I think the space will accommodate the new console model easily.'

Bart followed her across the dining room to the solarium. 'An excellent spot for a private studio! How lucky for you. I'm sure you'll have a full schedule of pupils in no time at all.'

'I hope so,' Sandy replied. 'I want to make a success of this business.'

Bart studied the room thoughtfully and measured some sections with a steel pocket tape. 'Now, I think that if the spinet were placed against the wall, and if those two chairs were taken out, we could move the new piano in right next to the music cabinet. What do you think?'

'Perhaps you're right,' Aunt Lotia agreed. 'We could remove the lamp table and magazine holder, too. They're just cluttering up the room.'

'Let's try it that way,' Bart suggested. 'But not now! Don't you two touch a thing. I'll have my men out here early tomorrow morning. They'll take care of everything. They have the proper equipment, and they've been trained to move heavy furniture.'

'How can we ever thank you!' Aunt Lotia exclaimed. 'I'm sure the use of your piano will be an important factor in the success of Sandy's recital.'

'The point is, how can *I* thank you!' Bart turned. 'Towner's Mart is sure to profit.'

The three of them sat in the living room and visited for a few minutes, then Aunt Lotia excused herself on the pretext of being tired. Sandy wasn't worried; Aunt Lotia had always been one to retire early.

'Sandy, would you like to go out and see the town?' Bart asked. 'Brunston doesn't offer a very gay night life, but we could take in a movie and maybe go to the Roundtable and dance. There's live music there almost every night.'

'I'd like that,' Sandy said. 'Is it all right with you, Aunt Lotia? You leave the dinner things.

41

I'll clean up the kitchen tomorrow.'

'Go, go, of course you must go,' Aunt Lotia said. 'I'll not have you sitting around here pretending to look after me. You young folk run along and have some fun.'

Sandy excused herself long enough to freshen her make-up and change into a pair of dressier shoes. A strange excitement filled her at the thought of going out with Bart Towner, but as she left the house she had the odd feeling that someone was watching them. Was Aunt Lotia staring after them, or was Dave at the ballroom window? Sandy forced herself to keep her eyes straight ahead as she slid onto the sleek leather seat of Bart's convertible.

CHAPTER FOUR

On the drive downtown Sandy felt as if she were on exhibit for the people of Brunston. Bart said he was driving slowly so that the wind wouldn't blow her hair, but he was constantly changing traffic lanes, as if trying for a better position. On the sidewalk passersby stared. Sandy felt that they were looking at her, but she tried to relax by telling herself that they were entranced with Bart's eye-catching car.

None of the theaters was showing pictures that appealed to Bart, and Sandy had never been a movie fan, so she didn't mind when they drove through the downtown business district and headed for the highway.

'How about a little music?' Bart tilted his head and looked at Sandy in the same appraising manner she had seen him use on the young couple buying furniture.

'I'd love to.' Sandy ignored Bart's gaze and tapped her foot to the music playing on the car radio. But she wondered why he was taking the long route to the Roundtable.

'I'm showing you off,' Bart said, as if reading her mind. 'I want Brunston to notice you. It isn't every night that I go out with such a beautiful girl.'

'Nor I with such a handsome man,' Sandy countered, determined not to trip over Bart's line. A young businessman like Bart probably had a large assortment of girl friends and scads of dates. He was just trying to make her feel special. And he had succeeded. Sandy felt like a princess going to a ball.

Inside the Roundtable a blue haze of smoke hung near the ceiling, and the room felt stuffy and hot in spite of the air conditioning. A piano and drum combo played the latest tunes from a spotlighted podium.

Bart found a booth away from the music where they could be alone and talk, but he spent plenty of time on the dance floor. He was a smooth dancer; Sandy hadn't expected anything else. A date like Bart Towner could almost make her forget about independence and a job in Chicago.

'I hope you're going to manage your piano studio on a businesslike basis,' Bart said as they relaxed in their seats between dances.

'I plan to,' Sandy replied. 'But I have no business experience. I've never done anything like this before, so I hardly know where to begin. I'm open to any suggestions you might care to offer.'

'Begin with a set of rules,' Bart said. 'Rules for your students that must be respected. If you let them know where they stand right from the beginning, you'll avoid misunderstandings later.'

'But what sort of rules do I need?' Sandy asked. 'I plan to give thirty-minute private lessons. I think any longer time than that would tax their attention span. Of course I plan to stick to a rigid time schedule. What other rules are there?'

'Those are your personal rules,' Bart explained. 'And they are good ones. But I mean that you're going to have to make rules for your pupils.'

'Like—be on time,' Sandy suggested.

'That's good for openers.' Bart paused as the waitress brought them sandwiches and coffee. 'But remember that you'll need to start out with a clear understanding of the financial arrangements involved. This is the potential danger area in any business deal. You must insist that your students pay by the month, and they must pay in advance. Allow no cancellations. Give make-up lessons only for sound reasons.'

'But is that fair?' Sandy asked. 'I suppose the pay-in-advance idea is okay, but no make-ups? No cancellations? Emergencies do arise. No one's immune. What if someone is sick on his lesson day?'

'Then that's tough,' Bart said. 'You'd be surprised how much lesson-day sickness can be traced to a poorly prepared lesson. I know that from my own experience. I had regular attacks of lesson-dayitis. Once the kids and their parents realize that you're no soft touch, they'll be consistent in their attendance.'

'You sound ruthless,' Sandy said with a laugh. 'I don't know if I can set up such rigid rules.'

'I'm a businessman.' Bart shrugged. 'As a businesswoman you'll have to look out for Number One. Nobody else will. It's easier to set the rules right at the start than to have to establish them later when a bad situation arises. Of course, if a kid has his arm in a cast, you might be lenient.'

'I should hope so.' Sandy laughed. 'I don't want the kids to think they're taking lessons from the Wicked Witch of the West.'

'It's no laughing matter.' Bart sipped his coffee. 'If you're serious about making a go of your studio, you'll have to allow yourself an enemy or two. You're on your own, you know.

There are no fringe benefits. You'll have no two-week vacation with pay. Nor will you have sick leave or paid holidays. When you don't teach, you don't get paid. It's as simple as that.'

Sandy folded accordian pleats into her napkin. 'I suppose you're right, Bart. There are only a few hours each week when students are available for private lessons. Private teachers have to make the most of them.'

'Right.' Bart pounded the table to emphasize his point. 'Now you're talking sensibly. When a student signs up for lessons, he's buying a chunk of your time. He's obligated to pay for it whether or not he chooses to use it. If someone doesn't come for a lesson, there's not too much you can do with that thirty-minute period. It's just a loss to you.'

Sandy sighed. She hadn't realized that she was going to have to be such a tough businesswoman. But common sense told her that Bart's ideas were sound. She wanted to be independent and self-supporting. And there was also Aunt Lotia's operation to consider. She sighed again.

'How do you think I should go about setting up these rules?'

'I'd write up a form letter and have it mimeographed,' Bart said. 'Just give a copy to each prospective pupil before you schedule him into your teaching day. And don't worry.

The parents will respect you for respecting yourself. Nobody appreciates anything that comes to them too easily.'

'You do make sense, Mr. Towner,' Sandy admitted with a grin. 'I'll start working on a letter first thing tomorrow. Aunt Lotia will probably help me with it. She always has good ideas.'

Bart rose. 'Enough business talk for one night. How about a little more dancing?'

Sandy felt as if she were floating in Bart's arms as they swirled from one side of the dance floor to the other. During one number everyone left the area, and she and Bart were the only performers. The musicians played three extra choruses of the tune, and when they stopped, everyone clapped and whistled. Bart bowed, whisked Sandy off the floor, and led her outside.

'They're all wondering who my beautiful date is.' Bart laughed as he drove from the parking area and turned the convertible onto the highway. 'I'll keep them in the dark for a while. Do you enjoy being a woman of mystery?'

'Oh, Bart, you're just teasing,' Sandy said. 'Everyone was admiring your dancing, not your date.'

By the time Bart took her home, Sandy was captivated with his good looks, his charm, and even his solid common sense. As she hurried upstairs to her room, she wondered how Dave could have been so mistaken about Bart. He wasn't arrogant or supercilious. Maybe Dave was just jealous of him.

Bart was excellent company, and Sandy hoped to spend other evenings with him. Living in Brunston was going to be more interesting than she had imagined.

*   *   *

The next two weeks flew by in a whirl of activity. Sandy spent endless hours at the piano, and more hours at the sewing machine making herself a special black chiffon dress and trying to design a scarf for Aunt Lotia that would hide some of her scars.

Bart called her frequently, and when she could spare the time, she went out with him. He seemed as interested in her new career as she was.

Dave asked to do sketches of Sandy as she practiced. At first she hadn't liked the idea. She thought it would make her so self-conscious that her practice would be meaningless. But Dave was so quiet that she hardly knew he was in the room. Some of his sketches were really good. She thumb-tacked one of them to the bulletin board in her room, and Aunt Lotia had one framed for the solarium. Sandy had always thought that sketching would be fun, but she had never taken the time to try it.

On the first of September the smell of fall was already in the air. Sandy could hardly believe that she was dressing for the recital. But the time had arrived. Aunt Lotia and Grace Cantrell had spent the day arranging huge baskets of chrysanthemums and marigolds to decorate the stage at the art center, and Aunt Lotia had matched candles to her flowers and created a breathtaking centerpiece for the tea table.

Bart asked to drive Sandy to the art center, but she gently refused. She wanted to go with Aunt Lotia, and, of course, Aunt Lotia invited Dave to share the back seat. They entered the red brick building through a rear door, and Sandy retired to a practice studio while Aunt Lotia and Dave took seats out front.

From the backstage studio Sandy could hear the murmur of the crowd and could smell perfume in the air. She practiced some warm-up drills as she waited for curtain time. Nerves prompted her to keep licking her lips until the taste of lipstick called her attention to the habit. She hastily repaired her make-up and took three deep breaths to steady herself.

Of course she was excited. She knew she wouldn't do her best if she weren't a bit keyed up. But she was smart enough not to confuse her excitement with fear. Her piano instructor at college had explained to her that this excitement was pure pent-up energy, to be used to advantage as she needed it.

Promptly at eight o'clock, the velvet curtain rose and Sandy stepped onto the stage. For an instant she heard the flutter of programs, then applause burst forth. Aunt Lotia's Wednesday Music Club had come through for her. The small auditorium was completely filled, and several people were standing by the doorway.

Sandy sat down at the piano, adjusted the bench, then began to play. Her nerves steadied, and she pretended that she was playing in the privacy of the solarium. The group of Bach preludes went well, and she followed them with a taste of Scarlatti.

After these numbers, Sandy could sense the audience beginning to warm up, and by the time she finished the Brahms Rhapsody, she knew she was being well received. She held her audience spellbound.

At intermission she retired backstage and saw no one by her own request. She drank a glass of ice water someone had thoughtfully provided, but she couldn't relax, and soon the intermission was over.

Beethoven, Chopin, Grieg—the piano keys seemed to come alive under her fingers. Before she knew it, she had come to the end of her original sonata.

The recital was over. After the applause died down, Sandy took her place in a reception line to greet her admiring audience. Everyone was lavish in his praise.

Sandy wished she knew a hundred different

ways to say thank you, because she felt that she was overworking the two words. Most of the people in the reception line were friends of her aunt's, but suddenly Sandy recognized a high-school classmate.

'Betty Blue!' Sandy exclaimed, greeting a sandy-haired girl. 'How good to see an old friend! And how nice of you to take the time to come here tonight.'

'I enjoyed every minute of it,' Betty replied. 'You couldn't have kept me away. I've always wanted to play the piano. Took lessons as a kid, but of course Mom couldn't get me to practice.'

'Maybe we can get together for a visit,' Sandy suggested. 'Could you come over to Aunt Lotia's for coffee and cookies some morning?'

Betty shook her head. 'Afraid not. I have a three-year-old girl and a set of one-year-old twin boys. I don't get out much during the day. But Hank's good to look after the kids in the evening. Maybe some night?'

'We'll see,' Sandy said. 'I'll call you.' Sandy really intended to call Betty, but somehow she knew from their brief meeting that they had little in common. She could hardly imagine being married, much less being tied down with three babies. A private meeting with Betty might find them with little to talk about.

In spite of the crowd, in spite of her successful performance, Sandy found her thoughts drifting to the job she had given up. In Chicago she would have had other teachers for friends, other young people who cherished independence and whose interests matched her own. Bart's light touch on her elbow brought her back to the present.

'May I see you home?' he asked. 'I'm not rushing you. I just want to get my bid in.'

'Thank you, Bart, but Aunt Lotia must be my escort tonight. Please understand. I feel pulled in two directions. You've gone out of your way to be kind and helpful, but this recital was Aunt Lotia's idea. She's slaved to make it a success. I don't want to leave her alone tonight.'

'If you're worrying about me, just forget it,' Aunt Lotia said. 'I overheard your talk. You two go on together.'

Sandy hesitated.

'Seems to me your aunt has an escort.' Bart nodded toward Dave, who was bringing Aunt Lotia a cup of punch and an assortment of cookies.

'Well . . .' Sandy grinned. 'You've both talked me into it. Dave will take care of you, Aunt Lotia. The crowd's thinning out, and I believe I met and talked with everyone. Let's wait just a few more minutes. After a few more people leave, I'll thank Grace Cantrell once more, and we'll be on our way.'

Later, at Sandy's request, Bart took her straight home. Somehow she felt that to go anywhere else would be anticlimactic. And Bart seemed to share her feeling.

They sat in the open convertible and talked for a long time. The moon hung like a silver ball against the black velvet of the sky, and the stars looked close enough to be touched. Sandy knew she would never forget such a beautiful night. When Bart walked her to the door, she turned to say good night and was not surprised when he gave her a kiss that sent her floating up the stairs to her room.

It was sometime later that Sandy realized she was still too excited to sleep. Getting up, she slipped into shorts and a shirt and went outside to sit on the balcony. This time it was Dave who called to her.

'I hardly got a chance to tell you that I enjoyed your music,' he said. 'But it was great. You're on your way toward making a name for yourself.'

'Thanks, Dave. The audience was wonderful. In fact, everything about the entire evening was great!'

'Including Bart Towner?' Then, when Sandy didn't answer immediately, he apologized. 'Sorry. Your private life is none of my business. I won't pry again. Sandy, how did you get to enjoy classical music? I mean, did you have to learn to like it? Or were you born with a silver clef in your mouth?'

'I'm not sure what you mean.' Sandy paused. Music was such a part of her that she found Dave's question hard to answer. 'I guess I've just always liked the classics, or any good music.'

'Wish I understood it,' Dave grumbled. 'That must be the first step toward liking it. It's impossible to like something you don't understand.'

'But you just told me you enjoyed the recital. Were you kidding me? Are you trying to tell me now that you really didn't care for my selections?'

'I enjoyed the recital because you were playing,' Dave told her. 'But the music was way above me. Some of it seemed to go on and on.'

'How did you get to the point where you enjoyed good art?'

'By being exposed to it, I suppose,' Dave said. 'I never thought much about it.'

'Same thing with me and music,' Sandy pointed out. 'Let's try an experiment. I'll loan you a recording of a Brahms symphony to listen to. I'll bet I can have you humming the main themes in less than a week. Of course, you must promise to cooperate. You have to want to learn to like it. That's half the battle.'

'It's a deal,' Dave agreed. 'I have a record player of sorts up here and a fresh needle or two. What do I have to do? Am I supposed to listen to the record for so many minutes each day or each week?'

'Never. That's the worst way to learn to enjoy any music. You can't force yourself to like a thing.' She stepped back into her room and returned in a few minutes with the record album.

'Just play this as background music while working—painting, preparing your schoolwork, anything. I think you'll be surprised at what will happen in a very short time.'

Dave took the record and thanked her, and they both retired to their rooms. Sandy was feeling drowsy now that she had come down from the cloud to which her performance had floated her. The recital had been wonderful. But had it served a real purpose, or had it just been an ego booster? Would private pupils materialize? Would she ever be independently self-supporting? The questions were still plaguing her as she finally fell asleep.

CHAPTER FIVE

By the time frost was crisping the October air, Sandy found her lesson schedule filling to capacity. She planned to teach five afternoons a week and part of the day on Saturday. Those were the times when the children were free of school responsibilities.

Sandy had followed Bart's suggestion for establishing rules, and to her surprise nobody had objected. Now, over their morning coffee, Aunt Lotia was beginning to express concern.

'Don't spread yourself too thin, Sandy,' she warned. 'A person can do just so much. I don't want you to have a breakdown from overwork.'

'That's unlikely,' Sandy laughed. 'I don't want to turn any students away. I can hardly believe that a few weeks ago I was worrying about having enough pupils to fill my time.'

'I think seven o'clock in the evening is a fair cut-off time.' Aunt Lotia poured them both another cup of coffee and passed Sandy a plate of cinnamon toast. 'If you start teaching promptly each afternoon at three, that gives you four full hours of work a day. That's enough.'

'I could do five,' Sandy said. 'I could do five easily. That would only include ten lessons.'

'Let's hold it to four,' Aunt Lotia insisted. 'Dave has hinted that he would rather you didn't teach after seven o'clock. And I can see his point of view. People coming and going do create some disturbance. I'd hate to lose Dave as a tenant. It's not so much the money he pays as it is his contribution to running the house. Don't know where I'd find another helper as willing and as dependable as he is.'

Sandy nodded and hid her surprise. She could hardly believe the first part of what her aunt had said. Dave objecting to her teaching? How could he! Surely he could hear little of the playing up in his third-floor quarters. Before Sandy could comment or ask questions, her aunt had changed the subject.

'I suppose you've wondered why Towner's Mart hasn't called for their piano.'

'I certainly have.' Sandy cleared the table and began washing a few breakfast dishes. 'They must surely need it for display in the store. I mentioned it to Bart, but he didn't have much to say. You two aren't plotting some surprise for me, are you?'

'Bart's agreed to loan us the piano for as long as you are operating your private studio,' Aunt Lotia said, picking up a dish towel. 'He has sold two pianos already as a direct result of your recommendation. You should really be getting a commission on sales.'

'But I've recommended a piano to no one,' Sandy said. 'I don't understand it.'

'Perhaps you haven't talked to anyone about the piano,' Aunt Lotia said, 'but just the fact that you use the Towner's brand in your teaching speaks louder than any recommendation you could give. Bart Towner has a good deal going for him. Towner's Mart is profiting from your studio.'

'Good.' Sandy rinsed out the dishpan. 'I certainly don't want to be indebted to the Towners any more than I already am. Bart has done a lot to help me get started in this business. I don't want him to think I'm using him.'

Aunt Lotia's expression was inscrutable. When they finished doing the dishes, she rubbed a spicy-smelling ointment into the

57

angry scars on her face.

'Sandy, if I were forty years younger, I wouldn't mind being indebted to a boy like Bart Towner. I wouldn't mind one little bit.'

'You wouldn't try any matchmaking, would you?' Sandy gave her a horrified look. 'You really wouldn't dare. I won't stand for it.'

'And why would you need a matchmaker!' Aunt Lotia laughed. 'I'd say that you were doing very nicely on your own. But enough of that. I'm going to walk to the post office this morning. Must get some exercise before winter sets in and we are snowed under.'

Her aunt had slipped into a sweater and was out the door before Sandy could think of a response. She supposed that walking wouldn't damage her aunt's heart. Perhaps her own heart was the one that needed protecting. She had no intention of becoming emotionally involved with anyone this year. She had to prove herself to herself, to become independent before she would even think of love and marriage.

Although Sandy realized that she was only working part time, the days passed swiftly, like grains of sand flowing through an hourglass. One evening after she had finished teaching, and after she and Aunt Lotia had eaten a snack, Dave appeared at the living-room door.

'I need help, Sandy,' he said, and began whistling a melody that she recognized as an excerpt from Brahms. But suddenly he

58

stopped in midphrase with a helpless look on his face and shrugged.

'What comes next?' he asked. 'Remember the record you loaned me? I shouldn't have returned it so soon. That melody started running through my mind, but for the life of me I can't remember how it ends. It's driving me crazy.'

'I'll get the record,' Sandy said. 'I can't recall that exact spot, either. Aunt Lotia, do you mind listening to some Brahms?'

'Not at all,' her aunt replied. 'It will be a pleasure. I always enjoy good music.'

Sandy went to her room for the album, puzzled that her aunt hadn't used the unexpected break in their evening routine as an excuse to retire. But she hadn't, although she had seemed tired even before supper.

Returning to the living room, Sandy played the recording until they found the theme Dave had been whistling. They listened to it in its entirety. And Aunt Lotia listened with them. Sandy felt as if she were being chaperoned. Was Aunt Lotia still worrying about what the neighbors might think?

'You were right,' Dave said when the music ended. 'Brahms is beginning to make sense to me. A month ago it was just a hodgepodge of notes and chords, but now I can hear melodies and counter-melodies that I never noticed before. I'd like to borrow your recording again. Old Brahms sort of sneaks up on a person.'

'I never thought of Brahms as sneaky,' Sandy laughed. 'But if you say so, it must be true. Here, keep the record as long as you like.'

'How is your family, Dave?' Aunt Lotia asked, entering into the conversation now that the recording had ended.

'They're fine.' Dave grinned. 'The twins were elected cheerleaders for the football season, so the house is noisier than ever. My brother in high school plays in the school band. The music director is switching him from the clarinet to the baritone saxophone, and you've never heard such a racket as that thing makes. It's a real honker.'

'I'd like to meet your family sometime,' Sandy said. 'They sound great.'

'How about next Sunday afternoon?' Dave asked, leaping at Sandy's suggestion. 'I'm taking the kids on a picnic to the river. I'm going to do some sketching, and the twins want to try their hand at it, too. Why don't you and your aunt both come along with us? It won't be too long before the picnic season is over.'

'I'd love to come,' Sandy said, then she saw the disapproving expression on her aunt's face. What was wrong? Surely Aunt Lotia couldn't object to a Sunday picnic.

'Won't you come with us, Aunt Lotia?' Sandy asked. 'The outing would be good for you. You haven't been to the country in ages.'

Aunt Lotia sniffed. 'I'm really afraid that a picnic might be too much for my heart. I'm not as used to children and noise as I used to be. I'll just spend the afternoon alone, if you don't mind.'

Sandy felt strangely ill at ease. Had her aunt emphasized the word 'alone,' or had she just imagined it? Aunt Lotia had come close to being rude to Dave, for what reason Sandy couldn't fathom. She knew her aunt liked Dave. He did all sorts of chores for her, keeping the old house in good repair. Only last week he had volunteered to remove the screens and put up the storm windows. Surely Aunt Lotia didn't think the neighbors would gossip about Sandy and Dave enjoying a picnic.

'Dave, what do you think of the idea of my having some music-soirees?' Sandy asked, trying to change the subject to a topic that would meet her aunt's approval.

'Soirees? My, but aren't we fancy!' Dave smiled, but he didn't laugh.

'It's not so fancy,' Sandy replied. 'The word simply means a music party that is held at night. I thought the name itself might fascinate the children, and it's much too soon to think of having a regular recital.'

'It sounds okay to me,' Dave said. 'I suppose it would be good advertising for your studio, too. The word will get around. Especially the word "soiree".'

61

'I think it's a grand idea,' Aunt Lotia said, 'but you certainly don't need any more pupils.'

'Are you sure you wouldn't mind the noise?' Sandy asked Dave. 'The parties would have to be between eight and nine at night.'

'I hardly ever retire at that hour.' Dave looked puzzled, and Sandy felt the same way. Why would Dave object to her giving evening piano lessons and not mind a series of evening musicales?

Sandy glanced at her aunt, who suddenly went into a coughing spasm and excused herself from the room. Sandy followed her and got her a glass of water, then her aunt excused herself for the evening.

It was a few days after Sandy had scheduled her first evening musicale that Bart called and asked her for a date.

'I'm sorry I can't make it, Bart,' Sandy said. 'But I've had this party scheduled for several days. You're welcome to attend, if you'd like, but it wouldn't be fair to the children or their parents for me to cancel it at this late date.'

'You can't let this private studio take up all your time.' The coolness in Bart's voice blew like a winter wind over the telephone wire, and Sandy shivered in spite of herself. Up until now Bart had seemed enthusiastic about her work.

'I said I was sorry,' she repeated. 'We'll have to make it another time.'

'All right,' Bart replied. 'I hope my call

hasn't interrupted your teaching schedule.'

The next instant Bart had broken their telephone connection, and Sandy stood there holding the receiver while the dial tone buzzed in her ear. Was Bart jealous of her work? She couldn't believe that of him. He had been so helpful in every way.

But Sandy could believe that Bart was not used to being turned down by any girl for any reason. And she was even more sure of this when she saw him driving two different girls around Brunston in his convertible on separate occasions.

It's really none of my business, Sandy said to herself. She had no special hold on Bart Towner. They were just friends. She kept repeating the thought to herself until she had it memorized, but every time the telephone rang, she dashed to answer it, hoping to hear Bart's voice. And each time her hopes were quashed.

When at last Bart did call her again, Sandy accepted the date so quickly that she felt herself blushing in embarrassment. Why had she acted so eagerly! But when Bart came to the door to pick her up, she had regained her composure and was able to greet him casually.

'Care to go to a movie?' Bart asked. 'I don't know what's playing, but we can drive through town and take a look.'

'Whatever you say,' Sandy replied, wanting to spend the evening in whatever manner Bart chose. Just being with him again was enough for her. It didn't matter where they went.

'On second thought, how about a sandwich and a drink at the Roundtable?' Bart headed the convertible in that direction. 'It has lots of atmosphere, and it's quiet enough so we can talk. It seems as if I haven't seen you for ages. We need to catch up on things.'

'It *has* been a long time,' Sandy agreed. 'But I noticed that you haven't been pining away in solitude.'

'If you're referring to Sylvia and Sharon, they mean nothing to me.' Bart adjusted his gold silk tie and tilted his head to look at Sandy in his unique appraising way.

'Is that what you tell Sylvia and Sharon about me?' Sandy asked, teasing. ' "Oh, that's just Sandy Stafford; she doesn't mean a thing to me!" '

'You know I'd never say such a thing,' Bart retorted. 'But how'd we get on this subject, anyway? Tonight we're going to talk about you—about us. We'll have no arguments, no fussing.'

As they entered the dimness of the Roundtable, a couple waved to Bart and asked him to join them. Sandy veered in the direction of their booth, eager to meet Bart's friends, but he took her elbow and steered her in the opposite direction as he made a joking excuse to the couple.

'Who are they?' Sandy nodded toward

Bart's friends after they placed their order.

'Just a couple I know from the country club,' Bart said. 'Nobody special.'

While they waited for their food to arrive, Bart invited Sandy to the dance floor. The same blue haze hung near the ceiling, but tonight a vocalist with a guitar provided the music. And he was good. Sandy was exhausted after three numbers, but she danced four more just to please Bart.

The crowd was pleased, too, and when Bart and Sandy left the dance floor, they received a round of applause. Sandy wondered why she always seemed to be on exhibit when she went out with Bart. She felt under a tension and filled with an uneasiness that made it impossible for her to relax completely.

When their sandwiches arrived, Sandy's had catsup on it, which she had made a point of asking to be omitted.

'I'll send it right back to the kitchen.' Bart snapped his fingers, trying to catch the waitress's eye.

'Don't bother,' Sandy said. 'A little catsup won't hurt me.'

Ignoring Sandy, Bart called the waitress, returned the sandwich, and replaced Sandy's order. When the waitress left, he turned to face Sandy.

'You're going to have to learn to assert yourself, girl. Don't let people take advantage of you like that. She made a mistake; it's her job to correct it.'

'But I really didn't mind all that much. Really I didn't.'

'And you don't mind letting a bunch of kids take up all your evenings with their eternal piano playing. You don't mind spending all day every Saturday listening to lesson after lesson after lesson. How do you stand it?'

'But that's my job, Bart.' Sandy was surprised and indignant. 'Surely you know that. Surely you knew how it would be. I'm just thankful that the studio is a success. I was so worried that it wouldn't be.'

'Can't you see that you're being used? Your aunt uses you as a companion. Towner's Mart uses you for advertising its pianos, and I'm to blame for that. Your students use up your very life. Why don't you get out of this town, Sandy? You'll wither and die here with nothing more exciting to think about than a few piano pupils.'

'Bart!' Sandy exclaimed. 'What's come over you? I thought you were interested in my studio. You were so helpful, so full of ideas when things were still in the planning stage. I just don't understand.'

'Maybe I'm telling the truth for the first time,' Bart said with a shrug. 'And believe me, I wouldn't bother if you didn't mean something to me. At first you were just another pretty face, another person who could enhance my business position with your studio.

66

But that's past. You're a real person to me now, and I've been miserable these past few days without seeing you.'

'What about Sylvia and Sharon?' Sandy tried for a teasing touch again, but it was too late. Bart was in no mood for teasing.

'I was trying to make you jealous,' Bart admitted. 'A low trick, but I seem to be full of them.'

'It worked.' Sandy grinned. 'I hated the sight of another girl in your car.'

'I'm telling you one thing for sure. As soon as I make it big in this town, I'm getting out. I'm leaving Brunston and all its small-town gossip. And when I go, I want you beside me. I mean it, Sandy. We'll ditch this town together.'

'Bart, I have a headache. Please take me home.' Sandy was too startled at Bart's sudden about-face to know what to say to him. One minute he was ignoring her, the next instant he was—What was he doing? He hadn't proposed. He hadn't said, 'I love you.' Just what had he said? His words had been filled with jealousy, with bitterness, a bitterness that Sandy didn't understand and didn't want to share.

Once Bart had left her at the front door, Sandy dashed upstairs before she had to face Aunt Lotia. Her aunt had taken to waiting up for her after her dates, and she couldn't explain something to her aunt that she couldn't explain to herself. Bart Towner was an enigma.

As she lay in bed, she mulled over Bart's words. Was she withering away here in Brunston? She hadn't thought so. Starting the studio had been a challenge, but she did realize that she was only working on a part-time basis. And that worried her. There must be something more she could do to be a functional, professional musician. But what was it? What could it be?

CHAPTER SIX

Sun streaming through her windows awakened Sandy on the Sunday morning of Dave's family picnic. Church bells chimed, and the promise of Indian summer hung in the air as she dressed and hurried to the kitchen to make a batch of caramel bars for their afternoon outing.

The whir of the electric beaters masked her aunt's footsteps, and Sandy jumped, startled to realize she was not alone. Aunt Lotia was usually an early riser, but today one look at her told Sandy that something was wrong. Aunt Lotia was still in her robe and slippers. Her shoulders were stooped, and instead of combing her hair, she had merely tucked it under a net.

'What is it, Aunt Lotia?' Sandy poured the

batter into a pan, then gave her aunt her full attention. 'Aren't you feeling well this morning?'

'Oh, I'm sure it's nothing,' Aunt Lotia said, reaching for the coffeepot. 'Just sort of a dizziness keeps coming over me, but I know a cup of coffee will fix me up.'

Sandy pulled out a chair and motioned her aunt into it. 'I'll make breakfast for you. You just sit there and take it easy for a while. Perhaps we should call Dr. Ward.'

'Nonsense,' Aunt Lotia replied. 'Nonsense and fiddlesticks! I'll not be bothering any doctor on Sunday morning.'

As soon as the coffee had perked, Sandy filled their cereal bowls and joined her aunt at the table. They lingered over breakfast, but as Sandy cleared the dishes away, she could see that her aunt felt no better. It was hard to tell whether she was pale or whether the lack of make-up just made her seem whiter than usual.

Sandy settled her aunt on the living-room sofa with the Sunday papers and hurried upstairs to straighten her room. When she came down later, her aunt seemed no better. She sighed and yawned and made no motions toward getting dressed.

'Perhaps we'd better skip church today,' Sandy said. 'You just settle back and rest. I'll fix us a light lunch later, and we'll spend a quiet day right here at home. You've probably been working harder than you should. Dr. Ward should know that you don't understand how one goes about taking it easy.'

'But this was the day Dave promised you a picnic, wasn't it?' Aunt Lotia murmured. 'I'll not have you missing out on your fun for my sake. Not for one minute.' She sighed again. 'You young people go right ahead with your plans.'

Sandy fought to keep the disappointment from her voice. 'Dave has a carload of brothers and sisters to picnic with. He'll never miss me. I'll send the caramel bars along with him, but I'll stay right here at home. You might need me for something before the day is done.'

Sandy brought her aunt a light wrap to throw across her legs, then she climbed to Dave's apartment to give him the bad news. She was surprised at her reaction to Aunt Lotia's setback. She had really counted on this picnic, this day with Dave and his brothers and sisters, more than she had realized.

Knocking on Dave's door, Sandy received no answer. 'Dave, are you there?' Still no answer. A glance out the window told her that Dave's old jalopy wasn't in the driveway. He had probably left by the back stairs and driven to Janesville to pick up his siblings. Sandy sighed. It could have been a great day.

Later in the morning, as Sandy was serving orange gelatin and toast to her aunt, they heard a knock on the door.

'That must be Dave,' Sandy said. But when she answered the knock, the ample form of their neighbor, Grace Cantrell, filled the doorway. Sandy stepped back, and Mrs. Cantrell walked in just as if she lived there.

'Just stopped by to see what on earth ails Lotia.' Mrs. Cantrell's voice matched her figure, and she entered the living room uninvited. 'It's not like Lotia to miss church. Not like her at all. I just said to myself, "I'll stop by and see what ails that woman."'

'Come in, Grace,' Aunt Lotia said, although Grace was already in. 'There's nothing wrong with me, but it's good of you to check up on me.'

'That's what neighbors are for,' Grace boomed. 'But you do look a bit down at the corners. Stomach upset?'

As the two women were chatting, Dave's car pulled into the driveway. Shouting and laughter filled the air.

'What on earth is going on?' Mrs. Cantrell asked. 'This used to be a quiet, dignified neighborhood.'

'It's just Dave,' Sandy explained. 'The young man upstairs. He has his brothers and sisters with him, but they won't stay long. We were going on a picnic today, and I haven't had a chance to tell him that I've changed my plans.'

'Sandy's such a dear,' Aunt Lotia said, not urging Sandy to go ahead with her plans. 'She insists on staying here with me this afternoon.

On a beautiful day like this it's really a shame.'

'A shame?' Grace Cantrell slapped her knee. 'It's utter rubbish, that's what it is!' She began plumping pillows, straightening the afghan, and picking up newspapers. 'Utter rubbish! Sandy, you go on with your young man. No sense in your wasting your day here when you can be off having fun. I'll stay with Lotia. I'd love to do it. I was just going to spend a lonesome Sunday at home, anyway. Now you scoot. Go on!'

Sandy didn't know what to say, and she couldn't seem to read the expression on her aunt's face. Was it surprise? Bewilderment? Or was it plain displeasure? Sandy wished she could talk to her aunt privately, but she knew that such a request would wound Grace Cantrell's feelings.

'Run along, Sandy.' Aunt Lotia's voice sounded high and strained, but she was smiling. 'You run along. Grace and I will get along just fine.'

'Coming, Sandy?' Dave called from the front door. 'Let's get this gang on the road before the neighbors call the riot squad.'

'Give me a minute.' Sandy dashed upstairs and changed into blue jeans and a faded sweatshirt; then, racing back to the kitchen, she picked up the caramel bars, waved good-bye to her aunt and Grace Cantrell, and hurried out to Dave's car. She grinned as she eased into the back seat with the twins.

72

'Meet the gang,' Dave said above the confusion. 'Hal and Guy up front and Vana and Lana in the back. You can ride herd on them for a while.'

Sandy slammed the car door after the greetings were exchanged and wondered how Dave told the twins apart. They were identical down to the parts in their blonde hair. One of the girls took the caramel bars and put them on top of a picnic basket.

'We packed the lunch,' the other twin said. 'Milk, cheese, hard rolls, and apples.'

'You can tell that they've been slaving over a hot stove all morning,' Guy said with a laugh. 'They're practically worn out before the picnic is under way.'

'He's a senior,' the first twin, Lana, said with a shrug. 'He has to act disdainful. It's an unwritten rule. Or maybe it's written down somewhere. Who knows!'

Dave was just easing out of the driveway when Bart pulled up to the front of the house.

'Ah-ha,' Dave whispered. 'A gentleman caller. We'll wait while madam speaks to him. But make it snappy. That guy's double trouble.'

Sandy crawled from the crowded sedan and walked to where Bart had stopped. The top to the convertible was down, and Bart made a handsome picture in a black and tan sports outfit that matched the interior of the car.

'I've come to rescue the damsel in distress,'

73

Bart said. 'Ditch that noisy gang and we'll drive to Des Moines. I have tickets for *Hawaiian Holiday.*'

'Bart!' Sandy cried. 'I wish you had asked me sooner. I really can't go to Des Moines with you. Dave's been wanting me to meet his family for ages. We're going out to the river on a sketching picnic. I can't back out now.'

'You mean you don't want to back out, isn't that it?' Bart's tone was curt, and his whole face stiffened in a masklike hardness.

'Perhaps you're right at that,' Sandy said, matching Bart's mood. 'Why should I want to back out on Dave? But if you'd care to join us, I'm sure we could make room for one more.'

'Thanks, but no, thanks.' Bart gave a bitter laugh. 'I've better ways to spend a Sunday afternoon than playing with children.'

The convertible tires squealed as Bart shot away from the curb and skidded around the corner. Sandy bristled. Bart had no right to demand her time at a moment's notice. But as she watched him speed off, she almost felt sorry for him. He seemed so alone, so very alone.

'In his usual even-tempered mood, I see,' Dave said as Sandy got back in the car. 'Angry.'

Sandy didn't reply, and an uneasy hush fell over everyone until the twins began practicing their cheerleading yells. Sandy was relieved in spite of the noise.

Although Sandy knew that Grace Cantrell

74

was at the house, she felt a bit guilty about leaving her aunt, and although she had no previous date with Bart, she hated to see him so upset with her. The afternoon was off to a dismal start.

Sandy's feelings churned until Dave turned into a shaded country road. The tires threw up a screen of dust that seemed to separate Sandy from her troubles. She relaxed. And by the time Dave stopped the car in a wooded river glen, she was ready to enjoy the scenery and the picnic.

In the distance Sandy heard the rush of water, and underfoot dry leaves crunched like potato chips. The pungent smell of fall was in the air.

'We always eat first,' Hal, the youngest boy, informed her. 'It's a rule.' He lifted the picnic hamper from the car as if it contained crown jewels.

'That's Hal's rule,' Guy said. 'I think the kid has a hollow leg.'

The twins spread out two cotton blankets on the grass, then opened the lunch basket. Sandy was surprised at how delicious dry rolls and cheese could taste. They took their time eating, and Sandy's caramel bars made a perfect dessert to go along with the milk.

'Maybe you should have brought a cow,' Sandy laughed as she counted the cartons of milk on hand. But somehow most of them were emptied before the meal ended. She grinned. She had never known such an easygoing, fun-loving family.

After lunch had been cleared away, the Miller clan followed their own individual pursuits. Guy hiked off to gather twigs and leaves for a school biology project. Hal pulled a fishing rod and a tackle box from the depths of the car trunk and streaked toward the river. And the twins and Dave brought out sketching boards, paper, and charcoal.

'Want to try your hand at some sketches?' Dave invited Sandy. 'We have plenty of supplies.'

'I can't even—'

'Draw a straight line,' the twins chanted in unison with her, and they all laughed.

'That's what everyone says,' Vana told her. 'But if you'll examine most sketches, you'll find that not too many straight lines are required. Give it a try and see what happens. You may be good at it.'

Sandy accepted the sketching equipment and sat down in a spot that gave her a perfect view of a small country church. Surely she could sketch those simple lines. As the twins wandered off to find their own special scenes, Dave showed Sandy how to hold the charcoal sticks and apply them to the coarse, heavy paper.

They worked silently for several minutes, then Sandy showed Dave the beginning of her sketch.

'Not bad,' Dave said. 'Not bad at all. I think you may have some hidden talent.'

Sandy grinned. 'It wasn't as hard to do as I thought it might be, but I'll bet you flatter all your pupils.'

'As a matter of fact, I do.' Dave went on talking and sketching. 'All kids need confidence. They try to act big and swaggering and important, but deep down they need someone to assure them that they're worthwhile people. They need to know that they're important in the scheme of things.'

Sandy was surprised at the serious turn to Dave's talk, but she appreciated him more because he shared such private thoughts with her.

'Your brothers and sisters seem confident enough. Do you reassure them?'

'Mom does that,' Dave said. 'She's the one who taught me that it's necessary. She's the real strength in our family. Guess you don't know, but my dad's known as the town drunk in Janesville. Hasn't held a job for years. Mom has supported the family ever since I can remember, and now that I have a job, I'm going to take over as much responsibility as she'll allow me.'

'I'm sorry, Dave,' Sandy said. 'I had no idea that you had family difficulties. And there I was complaining to you about my minor problems—Aunt Lotia's illness, my altered plans. You had a right to be disgusted with me.'

'No right at all,' Dave said. 'Just because I have troubles doesn't mean I can resent people who don't. I'm sorry about that night. It was just that you brought things into such sharp focus with your talk of fairness that I was blinded for a moment. It isn't a fair world. Things aren't going to turn out all right.' Dave repeated Sandy's words as if he had memorized them. 'Most people don't like to say stuff like that out loud.'

'But you had answers,' Sandy said. 'Good, sound answers. I've thought a lot about them since that night. Freedom within restrictions—that's a big idea.'

They sketched in silence for several moments, then Dave glanced at Sandy's sketchboard again.

'I think you really do have a knack for sketching.' Dave got up in order to study her work more carefully. 'No kidding, Sandy. Have you ever thought of studying art?'

Sandy shook her head. 'I've never thought about it at all, and it's too late now.'

'It's never too late to learn something new. Remember Grandma Moses!' Dave stood back and squinted at his own sketch. 'Why don't you take an evening class in sketching through Brunston's adult education program? I teach a two-hour session each Tuesday night in the junior high art room.'

'You do? That would be sort of fun. It

would be a change from piano lessons and recitals. I may take you up on the offer. I'll have to talk it over with Aunt Lotia. Are you a hard taskmaster?'

'Absolutely.' Dave glared at her in mock seriousness. 'But I take a special interest in each of my pupils—especially the pretty ones.'

Dave suddenly had a very vulnerable look in his green eyes, and Sandy turned away in embarrassment. Then, glancing at her sketch, an idea popped into her head.

'Maybe I could be a church organist,' she said half aloud, gazing at the church she had just sketched.

'First an artist, then an organist.' Dave laughed. 'Your mind jumps about like a grasshopper. What next?'

'I'm serious, Dave. I'm not doing enough work to keep busy. And part-time work means a part-time salary. That church over there gave me the idea that maybe there's a congregation somewhere in Brunston that could use an organist. A job like that would be useful to the community, and it wouldn't interfere with my private-studio schedule. I'm going to check into it just as soon as I get home. Don't know why I haven't thought of it sooner. I've had lots of organ lessons.'

Sandy made her decision just as Dave's brothers and sisters returned, bringing noise and laughter along with them. Everyone helped repack the car, and it was dusk as they drove into Janesville.

Dave delivered his family to what seemed to be a deserted frame house; then, in the relative silence, he drove back to the Stafford home.

'It's been a wonderful day, Dave,' Sandy said earnestly. 'Really wonderful. I wouldn't have missed out on it for anything.'

CHAPTER SEVEN

There were eight churches in Brunston, and within a period of a few days Sandy made appointments to talk to and to perform for the organist of each one. Knowing that the position of church organist was a demanding one, she offered her services as a substitute musician on those special occasions when the regular organist might like to have a Sunday away from the keyboard.

'My dear, you are heaven-sent!' Mrs. Ludwig exclaimed when Sandy finished playing an organ prelude and sight-reading a hymn. A spry sparrow of a woman, Mrs. Ludwig perched on the organ bench and showed Sandy some tricks about manipulating the stops of the Presbyterian pipe organ.

'My family's holding a reunion in the northern part of the state three weeks from Sunday, and I really would like to attend.

Would you be free to substitute for me on that day?'

Sandy searched in her purse until she found a small datebook, then she pretended to check the calendar. She didn't want Mrs. Ludwig to know that this would be her first job as organist.

'Yes, Mrs. Ludwig.' Sandy circled the date on her calendar and made a note in the margin of her book. 'I would be able to pinch-hit for you on that day. Will you give me instructions? Is there anything special to be included in the service on that date?'

'You're wonderful, Sandy!' Mrs. Ludwig handed Sandy a church bulletin. 'Here's our current order of service. You'll be expected to provide the usual. Prelude, hymns, responses, offertory, anthem accompaniment, postlude, and background music for seating late arrivals. We have lots of music in our files here, and you are welcome to use whatever you need. Think you can manage?'

'I'm sure I can.' Sandy tucked the bulletin into her purse, along with her datebook. 'Now, this job will involve accompanying a choir rehearsal, won't it?'

Mrs. Ludwig nodded. 'Thursday night at seven o'clock. But you won't have to stay for the whole rehearsal. Whenever you get here between seven and eight, we'll go over your number. I'll check with the choir director as to what it will be. He usually has the anthems scheduled six weeks in advance of performance.'

Sandy turned to leave the church. 'Thank you so much, Mrs. Ludwig. I appreciate the opportunity you have offered me, and I'll do my best to fill your place.'

Sandy soon heard different versions of the same story at the other churches she visited. The organists gave her a warm welcome and did everything except strew rose petals in her path. In Brunston, as in many communities, an organist-at-large was an unheard-of species. The regular organists often sacrificed personal pleasures in order to serve their churches. Sandy's Sunday schedule was filled well into December by the time she returned home.

'Aunt Lotia, you won't believe it! I already have six jobs lined up, and the organists made me feel as if I were doing them a personal favor by working for them. I can't understand why it took me so long to think of that idea. I could have been helping out all along!'

'But it will absolutely spoil your Thursday evenings,' Aunt Lotia pointed out. 'Better think that over carefully. Are you sure you want to get involved in such work?'

Sandy hung her coat in the closet. 'Of course I want to be involved. Anyway, it will only take a smidgen of time on Thursdays. You won't mind, will you? Of course, I won't leave you alone if you're feeling ill.'

'Goodness, child! I've been feeling fine. I

won't have you tailoring your evenings to suit me. Not for one minute. And if an emergency should arise, I can always call on Grace Cantrell.'

With a recipe book opened before her, Aunt Lotia was sitting at the kitchen table making a list of some sort. Sandy glanced over her shoulder.

'Don't tell me that's the grocery list!' Sandy exclaimed. 'We couldn't use all those things in a month.'

Aunt Lotia laughed and pointed to the calendar. 'I'm planning our Thanksgiving dinner, and none too soon at that. Do you realize that the Thanksgiving holiday is almost upon us? I have to issue our invitations and begin planning the menu.'

'Do you really think you're up to having all the relatives here this year? It's such a job. You work for days ahead. I remember that from years past. Of course I'll do all I can to help, but don't you think you should ask Dr. Ward's advice before you go ahead with more plans?'

'Dr. Ward is not managing my life,' Aunt Lotia retorted. 'He said I could continue my normal activities, that I'm just not to overexert. And Thanksgiving dinner is certainly one of my normal activities.'

'And I call preparing a feast for twenty-odd people overexerting.' Sandy shook her head and frowned. 'If you must go through with this, why not ask each of your sisters—all of the ladies, in fact—to bring her favorite covered dish? If everyone pitched in and furnished part of the food, your work load wouldn't be so heavy. Under the circumstances everyone would understand. They'd want to do their share.'

Aunt Lotia poured them both cups of coffee. 'I wouldn't even dream of doing such a thing. Thanksgiving dinner at my home is a tradition.'

'And so is Christmas dinner, Easter dinner, Fourth of July picnic, and any other holiday one can name. Why not let one of the others take a turn this time? It would be a nice outing for you to visit one of your sisters or brothers.'

Aunt Lotia shook her head, and her eyes blazed with blue fire. Even her smile vanished. 'I won't have it! My brothers and sisters are the only family I've ever had. It's one of the few pleasures in my life to entertain them royally at holiday times. Many of the women work, and I delight in giving them a real holiday.'

Sandy could understand her aunt's point of view. It was sad not to have any family of one's own. She certainly couldn't deny her aunt this pleasure so dear to her.

'I still say it wouldn't hurt any of them to bring something for the table,' Sandy repeated. 'I know they'd be more than glad to do it.'

'They'd suspect.' Aunt Lotia added sugar to her coffee and stirred it. 'None of them knows anything about my heart condition. And I'm doubly determined to keep it a secret. I won't have the whole family treating me like an invalid. I'll manage this dinner just as I've managed other dinners in the past.'

'*We'll* manage it,' Sandy corrected. 'Don't forget that I'm here to help. And we'll do it a little at a time. Many things can be prepared ahead of time and frozen.'

'You're right! We'll manage. I've already purchased the ingredients for my fruitcakes. I'm going to start mixing and baking today. Would you like to ask Bart to Thanksgiving dinner? Seems that I haven't seen much of him lately.'

'I'd rather ask Dave.' Sandy spoke before she thought.

'Why do you say that?' Aunt Lotia scowled. 'Dave has a huge family of his own close by. He doesn't need us. Now Bart—he has nobody but his father. We could invite Mr. Towner, too. One or two more won't make any difference.'

'Of course you're right. We should invite the Towners. It's just that Dave's so easy to be with, while Bart is so prickly.'

'Perhaps Bart wouldn't be so prickly if he didn't have such a hard time getting to see you. You're always having a musicale or dashing off to this new sketching class Dave's talked you into attending. And now you'll be tied up with choir practices on Thursday nights. I don't blame Bart for being prickly.'

'Put pickled peaches on that grocery list.' Sandy smiled to think that Bart's personality reminded her of pickled peaches. 'Bart loves them. I think the chef at the Roundtable keeps them on hand just for Bart.'

'But I have some jars of pickled peaches right here in my fruit cellar,' Aunt Lotia replied. 'Never did much pickling before. But I like to try something new each year. Keeps me young.'

Sandy was glad to end their conversation on a pleasant note, and as she left the kitchen she decided to ask Bart to Thanksgiving dinner sometime that very day. She would ask him early before he made other plans.

In the afternoon, before her pupils began arriving for their lessons, Sandy tried to telephone Bart. She hated to call him at Towner's Mart, but there was no other way to reach him. She needn't have worried. A voice on the other end of the line told her that Bart had gone to Chicago on a buying trip and wasn't expected back until that evening.

It was after supper before Sandy thought about Bart again. And it was too late to call him then. Dave was waiting to drive her to their sketching class. It was not exactly a date, but Sandy had welcomed his invitation to ride over together. Her sketching boards weren't heavy, but they were clumsy to carry. She appreciated Dave's thoughtfulness, and when they arrived at the schoolhouse, she made a habit of helping him carry his supplies and equipment to their classroom.

Sandy enjoyed the art lessons. The classroom held intriguing odors left over from the schoolday—turpentine, paint, chalk. The people she met were friendly. And the evening provided a welcome break in her musical work week.

'Your sketching is improving,' Dave said later that night as he added a few strokes to a tree and corrected some lines on a fence. 'I think you might begin trying to sketch the human figure. What do you think?'

'I could never do that,' Sandy protested. 'Still life and outdoor scenes don't move around. But humans . . .'

'Don't be negative,' Dave laughed. 'Of course you can do it. Pick someone here in the classroom, someone who works intently and who doesn't move around a lot. Give it a try. Do what you can, and I'll offer some suggestions later. You'll learn more by actually doing it for yourself than by reading about it in textbooks or being told what to do before you start.'

By the end of the class period, Sandy had sketched a rather grotesque likeness of Mrs. Wolfgang, the lady who sat across the aisle from her.

'Not very flattering, I must say.' Mrs. Wolfgang grinned at the sight of the sketch. 'I seem to have a big head. And I never realized that my arms were so uneven.'

Sandy tucked the sketch into her art folder. She had trouble keeping things in proportion as she sketched, but she hoped that Dave could help her out. She was waiting to ask him about it when Bart strode into the classroom.

'I just got back in town,' Bart announced. 'I'd like to have you join me for a snack, if you haven't promised your whole evening to Van Gogh.' Bart gave a condescending nod toward Dave.

'I tried to call you today.' Sandy smiled and ignored Bart's rudeness. 'I have something to ask you. I had no idea you were in Chicago. Wait a minute while I tell Dave I won't be going directly home.'

'How come that guy has to be in on all your plans, all *our* plans?' Bart demanded when Sandy returned. 'He really seems to rate with you for some reason.'

'I was only being polite.' Sandy shrugged into her coat, irritated that Bart was being so demanding. 'Dave is good enough to drive me to class, and I think he deserves to know that I'll not be riding back with him. Okay?'

'So okay.' Bart took her elbow and guided her to the door as if she couldn't find the way without his aid.

'Why don't you join this art class, Bart?' Sandy suggested. 'It's a relaxing way to spend an evening, and the people here really get to know one another. I've met a lot of new friends, people I would never have known otherwise.'

Bart shrugged. 'Who needs people? I meet hundreds of them every week at the store. Big deal!'

Sandy bristled, then she forced herself to calm down. Bart was a loner. Dave had told her that even before she started going out with Bart. Maybe Bart really didn't enjoy people. Maybe he had never had a chance to form close associations with others. Sandy remembered the family dinner. Maybe this was what Bart needed to soften him up a bit. Sandy didn't know how anyone could be a loner at a family dinner.

She inhaled the scent of the leather upholstery as Bart drove to his usual haunt, the Roundtable. How different Bart and Dave are, she thought with a smile. Their cars even smelled different. Dave's old jalopy was scented with turpentine, or perhaps an apple that someone had carelessly tossed on the floor. Bart's convertible seemed almost antiseptic by comparison. It still had that new-car odor, and the faint scent of Bart's lemony aftershave lotion only added to the impression of sleek suaveness.

Inside the Roundtable Bart nodded curtly to the people who greeted him, but he didn't pause for any idle chatter or friendly conversation. He propelled Sandy directly to their usual secluded booth in the corner. After coming in from the cold, the smoke and the sudden warmth of the room made Sandy's eyes water.

'You're crying,' Bart said. 'What's the matter? I expect my girl to smile when I get back in town.'

'I'm not crying.' Sandy wiped at her eyes with a tissue, not knowing whether to be irritated or pleased at being called Bart's girl. 'Why would I be crying?'

'Because you're stuck in Brunston, Iowa, with an elderly aunt and a bunch of sniffling kids you call pupils and who are using up your youth.'

Sandy chose to ignore Bart's barbed comments. He was just miffed because she had been at art class with Dave. She didn't even tell Bart about her success in getting appointments as a substitute organist. He wouldn't understand that, either. Instead of trying to explain her lifestyle to him, she came right to the point of the other matter on her mind. She would win Bart over to her way of thinking with understanding, not arguments.

'Bart, will you and your father share Thanksgiving dinner with me and Aunt Lotia and all our family? We'd both love to have you join us.'

'When is it?' Bart smoothed his tie and refused to meet Sandy's gaze.

'Bart! When do people usually have

Thanksgiving dinner? It'll take place sometime around noon on Thanksgiving Day.'

'I have a better idea,' Bart said. 'Dad's going to South Dakota to hunt pheasant, so count him out. Why not come with me to Chicago? I picked up a pair of tickets to the Brentwood Theater. We'll see a premier of *Once Last Autumn.*'

Sandy gasped. 'How did you ever get the tickets? Oh, Bart, you're just teasing me! No one can get tickets to that show unless they know the stars or something. You're teasing!'

'Of course I'm not teasing. Dad has important connections in Chicago. Getting tickets is no problem if your name's Towner. Come along with me. You need to get out of Brunston and see how the rest of the world lives.'

'But on Thanksgiving Day?' Sandy frowned.

'Why not? We can drive to Chicago early Thursday morning, have lunch in the Beach Room, see the play, and drive back here under the stars.'

Sandy was speechless. The day Bart outlined for her sounded magnificent. It sounded like Bart. Who else would make such plans for Thanksgiving Day? But what about Aunt Lotia's dinner? What about all the relatives who were coming? She couldn't just walk out on them at the last minute.

Suddenly Sandy felt her eyes watering again, and this time it wasn't from the cold.

'B-Bart, I can't go on Thanksgiving Day. I just c-can't.' She lowered her head and searched in her purse for another tissue.

'If you can't, you can't.' Bart's voice was matter-of-fact, and he ignored Sandy's tears. 'But I imagine I can find some other girl who can. Of course, I'd rather the girl were you.' He covered her hand with his, and Sandy felt a tingle clear up to her shoulder.

'Let me think about it, Bart.' Sandy sniffed and conquered her tears. There was really nothing to cry about. 'Give me a day or two to consider what I should do.'

CHAPTER EIGHT

Sandy waited several days before she even dared to tell her aunt about Bart's invitation. Bart was insisting upon an answer, and Sandy knew she had to make a decision soon. It was unfair of her to keep him dangling.

'But of course you must go to Chicago with Bart,' Aunt Lotia said. 'What a wonderful opportunity! And tickets to the Brentwood! How can you even think of turning him down?'

'I didn't dream that you'd want me to go,' Sandy said. 'What about the family? I was in summer school when everyone was here in July. I'll really miss seeing them. And what will they think about my deserting them for a day in Chicago? And what about you? You shouldn't try to handle that big dinner all alone. I simply can't let you do it.'

'Alone! Humph!' Aunt Lotia snorted. 'Grace Cantrell will be more than delighted to help me out. She told me just yesterday that her family's too far away to plan to get together for the holiday. I'm sure she'll enjoy being included in the Stafford household. And no one will think a thing about her helping me out a bit.'

'You make it hard for me to tell Bart no,' Sandy said. 'I really thought you'd object. I thought I would stay here with you as we had planned. I just don't know what to say. I'll really miss the family, but—'

'Couldn't help overhearing the talk,' Dave said, passing through the hallway on his way upstairs. 'If you're still lonesome for family after you get back from Chicago, just drive out to my house at Janesville. Mom and the twins serve midnight snacks from eleven until one. We'd all be glad to see you.'

'Thanks, Dave,' Sandy said. 'That's sweet of you. But there's really no family like one's own. I know you can understand that.'

Dave went on upstairs, and Sandy paced the living room. Why were decisions so difficult for her!

'Call Bart,' Aunt Lotia insisted. 'Call him right this minute. You're being unfair to keep him waiting so long for your answer.'

93

Sandy knew her aunt was right. Why had she delayed? Was it Aunt Lotia's disapproval she feared, or was it fear and dislike of the idea of Bart's taking some other girl to Chicago? Sandy's finger was like an icicle as she went out to the hall and dialed Bart's number.

'Bart? Sandy. I've decided to take you up on your invitation to go into Chicago on Thanksgiving Day. Aunt Lotia has excused me from the family gathering. Everything's set.'

'I thought you'd see it my way.' The warmth in Bart's voice flowed over the wire. 'I can't imagine anything more dismal than spending a holiday with a bunch of aunts and uncles. Can you be ready for an early start?'

'How early?'

'How about five o'clock? I know it's still dark then, but that should put us in Chicago by eleven. I've made reservations for lunch at the Beach Room. That sound okay to you?'

'Sounds as if you were pretty sure of yourself,' Sandy said with a laugh.

'And why not?' Bart chuckled. 'I knew I was going all the time. You were the one in doubt.'

Sandy hung up the receiver wondering why her talks with Bart always ended on a dissonant tone. Why did she have the feeling that Bart was trying to pressure her into his way of thinking?

Sometimes she told herself that she should stop seeing Bart entirely, that she should make a clean break. Dave was more her type. They seldom argued, and she could always relax with him. Then the next minute she would tell herself that she would be foolish to stop seeing Bart. He was handsome and good company. At times she even thought she might be falling in love with him. But she tried to check those feelings. She wasn't ready for love.

* * *

The few days before Thanksgiving dropped from the calendar like leaves in a high wind. Sandy helped her aunt get the house in tip-top shape. She froze salads, desserts, and breads, and Mrs. Cantrell agreed to come over early on Thursday morning to help stuff and roast the turkey.

There really was no reason for Sandy to feel guilty about going to Chicago, but she did. She couldn't help feeling that her true place was in Brunston with her relatives. Bart could have asked for tickets for any Sunday. Why had he chosen Thanksgiving Day?

On Thursday, Sandy was up at four o'clock, and by five she and Bart were speeding along the interstate. It was some time before Sandy could relax and put Aunt Lotia and the family gathering from her mind.

'You're awfully quiet,' Bart said. 'Sleepy? Or are you having last-minute regrets about being here?'

'I'm just thinking,' Sandy said. 'Three months ago I could hardly wait to go to Chicago, and now that I'm going there . . .'

'Life is full of ironic situations,' Bart said. 'It doesn't pay to look back. And sometimes it doesn't pay to look too far ahead. Just live for the day. Enjoy what you have and don't question it.'

Sandy took Bart's advice for that day, at least. She was out with the man of her choice, they were going to a sellout performance, and she intended to enjoy every moment of the day. But in spite of her intentions, everything seemed to remind her of someone at home.

The drive to Chicago passed quickly. Sandy was so busy peering at skyscrapers and into shop windows that she almost forgot how hungry she felt. They had not stopped for breakfast, so brunch was in order.

The Beach Room with its plush carpets and exotic decorations faded into the background as the waitress served them ham slices along with a pineapple salad. But all Sandy could think about was Uncle Jake trying to peel a fresh pineapple on one Thanksgiving when she had been a little girl. The unwieldy fruit had pricked his hands, and before he had conquered it, it had slid from its plate to Aunt Lotia's carpet. Sandy smiled at the memory.

'Like this place?' Bart asked, returning her smile. 'I think it's really neat. Dad and I always eat here when we come to Chicago on business.'

'You knew I'd like it,' Sandy told him. 'You have an intuition for such things.'

After their brunch Bart decided there was time to show Sandy around Chicago. Since he had parked the car for the day, he hailed a taxi for their brief tour. State Street, Michigan Avenue, Lakeshore Drive. Sandy saw all the places she had dreamed of. Five lanes of traffic flowed like a glittering ribbon, and their driver maneuvered his car smoothly and adroitly as he chewed on a stub of cigar that added to the air pollution.

After they dismissed the taxi, they walked a short distance to the theater. Sandy welcomed the chance to stretch her legs for a few minutes.

Once inside the theater, Sandy glanced around in surprise and amazement. She had expected an auditorium that would seat thousands. Instead, they were in a small theater that contained only a few hundred seats at the most.

'No wonder Chicago plays run for months on end,' Sandy remarked. 'Only a few people can see the performance at one time.'

'But the sound system is perfect,' Bart pointed out. 'That's one reason the theater is so small. Everyone here has a good seat because there aren't any bad seats. I like it this way. It makes a person feel rather special.'

The houselights dimmed, the curtain rose,

and Sandy prepared herself to enjoy the play, but somehow in the back of her mind lingered thoughts of Brunston. About this time Aunt Addie would be refusing dessert, and Uncle Will would be asking for a second scoop of ice cream on his pumpkin pie. And Aunt Cecile would be moaning about the mound of dishes to be washed.

Suddenly Bart laughed and nudged her, and Sandy snapped back to the present. She had missed a funny line. The whole theater was in an uproar, and the actors were improvising actions to allow time for the laughter.

'What's the matter?' Bart asked, still chuckling. 'Didn't you think that quip was funny? Aren't you enjoying the play?'

'It's great!' Sandy nodded and forced a smile, and to her relief the show went on. She glued her gaze to the stage and tried to pay attention. What ailed her? She reminded herself that she was seeing Chicago's best, but she was glad when the curtain rang down on the final act, glad when they were back in the convertible and on the highway leading to Brunston.

Darkness fell soon after they left Chicago, and Sandy rather dreaded the long ride ahead of them. She felt as if she had been sitting all day long. Sometimes when Bart was aloof and silent, she dozed. But much of the time he kept up an active conversation that required her attention.

'Do you really enjoy that sketching class?' Bart asked. 'Do you really think it's worthwhile?'

'I think it's great,' Sandy said. 'I wish you'd start coming to it. It would be a change for you. It would be something to take your mind off the furniture store and all your problems there.'

'Sketching's not for me,' Bart said firmly. 'And neither's Dave Miller. What a square! Of course, with his background, I suppose he can't help himself. I suppose he considers himself Bohemian. I don't see how you and your aunt can stand him around all the time.'

'I don't know what Aunt Lotia would do without him.' Sandy tried not to bristle at Bart's unfair remarks, and she didn't attempt to explain that Dave had risen above a trying family situation that would have broken a person with less character and determination.

'Dave's used to taking care of a big family. He does all the ordinary man-type chores, and he spots trouble before it has a chance to happen. We're lucky to have him with us.'

'Your aunt may need him,' Bart agreed, 'but I wish you'd stop seeing so much of him. How do you think it makes me look? I don't like to have my girl always hanging around some nutty artist.'

Sandy felt a rush of anger knot into a hard ball in her stomach, but she had no intention of ruining her day or Bart's. In a way she liked being called Bart's girl; on the other hand, she resented Bart's possessiveness. There had been no agreement between them to indicate that she was strictly his girl. She chose her words carefully.

'I'm afraid that I couldn't banish Dave from my life even if I wanted to. We do live in the same house, you know. But you needn't worry about him. He's just a good friend, or maybe I should say that he's just like a brother. I've never had a brother, you know.'

'Brother!' Bart spat the word. 'A lot you know about brothers! Don't ever say that word to me again.'

At first Sandy thought Bart was kidding her, but there was no mistaking the bitterness in his voice or the hardness in his face. Did Bart think her insincere? Surely he knew that she was an only child and an orphan. The knot of anger threatened to spill over, but she managed to hold it in check.

They drove for hours in silence, pausing only to fill up on gasoline, and when Bart stopped the convertible in front of her house, Sandy realized the extent of Bart's unexplained anger. He leaned in front of her and opened the car door without offering to walk her to the door.

Sandy got out of the convertible and dashed to her front porch. She fumbled in her purse for the door key, and by the time she had fitted it into the lock, Bart had driven on down the street. He hadn't even waited to see that she got inside safely.

The next day Sandy told Aunt Lotia all the pleasant things about her long day in Chicago, and in turn she heard all the details of the family Thanksgiving celebration. At ten o'clock they were still talking when the telephone rang. Sandy answered, and after a brief conversation she faced her aunt once more.

'Now what have you volunteered to do?' Aunt Lotia asked. 'I know that was someone wanting something.'

'That was a Mr. Rondee,' Sandy said. 'He asked me to tutor his daughter in music theory this weekend. She's enrolled at the university and is having trouble. Quarterly grades are almost due and she needs help fast. I told him I could see her tonight and again late tomorrow afternoon.'

'Sandy! Sandy!' Aunt Lotia shook her head. 'You're doing too much already. And now you've tied up your whole weekend.'

'He's going to pay me,' Sandy said. 'It's a job, and I can use the money. Part-time work means part-time pay. Wish I had thought of tutoring before. I might even offer an evening class in the basics of music theory.'

Aunt Lotia muttered and began peeling potatoes for dinner.

Upstairs in her room, Sandy mulled over her thoughts about a class in music theory. If

101

Dave could teach a night class, why couldn't she? Without saying any more to her aunt, Sandy made an appointment with Mr. Hays, the Brunston superintendent of schools. It wasn't until later that day, when she was sitting in Mr. Hays's waiting room, that she began to get nervous.

'Miss Stafford,' Mr. Hays said, shaking her hand. 'My wife heard your recital last fall and had nothing but good things to say about it. What can I do for you today?'

'I have an idea that I thought might interest you.' Sandy poured out her thoughts and plans before she lost her nerve. 'Brunston High surely has some students who are planning to major in music in college, or even some adults who are interested in knowing the basic techniques of sight reading, harmony, and keyboard chord constructions.'

'You seem to have a sound idea,' Mr. Hays said. 'We've never been able to offer music theory at the high-school level—just no room in the schedule. A night course in this area might be well received, and I'm sure you're qualified to teach this subject. Why don't I advertise such a course in our adult educational program for spring? If eight people sign up, we'll hold the class.'

'That will be wonderful. If there are enough people interested in the course, fine. If not, we'll just forget about it.'

'I think you'll get your class,' Mr. Hays

predicted. 'I've been hearing nothing but good comments about your private teaching, and I've heard you at the organ on two occasions. You have my support, and I wish you all success.'

Sandy was elated until she arrived home. She knew her aunt wouldn't approve of her taking on any new projects. She decided not to mention this new venture until she had to. But she needn't have worried. Aunt Lotia didn't even ask where she had been. Instead, she met Sandy at the door with news of her own.

'Bart called just a few minutes ago. You're to call him back the minute you can. You two didn't quarrel, did you?'

'It was nothing,' Sandy said. 'Just some sort of a misunderstanding. I'm really not quite sure what it was all about. I said something that upset him.'

Aunt Lotia left Sandy to place her call in privacy, but she knew her aunt was straining her ears from the kitchen. In a few moments Bart was on the other end of the line.

'Guess I owe you an apology,' he began. 'About yesterday. I'm sorry. I had no right to get so huffy. If you'll let me take you out to the Roundtable tonight, I'll make a formal peace offering.'

'Oh, Bart, you know I don't want any peace offering. And I'm sorry if I upset you yesterday. Our misunderstanding was partly my fault, I'm sure. But I can't go out tonight.

I'm tutoring a college student, and I have no idea how late we'll work.'

'How about after lessons tomorrow afternoon?' Bart asked.

Sandy sighed. 'Sorry. The same thing. This girl's about to flunk music theory. I couldn't turn her down. I just couldn't. Anyway, when I agreed to help her, I had no idea that you would ever speak to me again.'

There was a long silence, then Bart spoke in a tight, unpleasant voice. 'Sandy, will you put me down for a date on your calendar for January eighteenth? That should be far enough ahead to be a free evening. And I've checked it out. It falls neither on your sketching night nor on your choir rehearsal night.'

Sandy checked her purse calendar. Everything Bart said was true. However, January eighteenth was the night that Florence Carol was performing in the Brunston Community Concert series. Sandy had had her ticket for weeks.

'Bart—' She hesitated. 'Would you like to go to a concert with me on the eighteenth? Florence Carol, the Metropolitan soprano, is singing here that night. I can still get you a ticket through the concert board if you'll go with me.'

'Sorry.' Bart's tone was curt. 'This time I asked first. The eighteenth is the big monthly dance at the country club. I never miss attending those dances. You know how much they mean to me. Everyone in Brunston will be there.'

Sandy had no idea how much the monthly dances meant to Bart, but she gave in. She liked Bart, and he might never call her again if she turned him down this time.

CHAPTER NINE

Sandy had just finished her telephone conversation with Bart when someone knocked at the door. Peering through the window, Sandy saw a familiar figure on the front porch.

'Hello, Mrs. Ludwig.' Sandy ushered the birdlike lady into the living room.

'I'll get right to the point,' Mrs. Ludwig began, shaking her head to refuse the chair Sandy offered. 'I'm resigning as organist at the church, and since I'm chairman of the music committee, I've been appointed to ask you to take my place. Will you consider this, Sandy?'

Sandy persuaded Mrs. Ludwig to have a chair, then she seated herself on the sofa near her.

'You want me to take the job permanently?' Sandy asked. 'You mean I'd be full-time organist?'

Mrs. Ludwig nodded. 'The committee

would like you to serve on a trial basis through the advent season, but I'm sure your work will be satisfactory. It's just a precaution the music committee always takes before they hire anyone. It will be a great relief to me if you accept the job.' Mrs. Ludwig sighed. 'I've played that organ almost every Sunday for twenty-five years. I'm more than ready for a break.'

'I'll be happy to try to fill your place,' Sandy said without hesitating. 'It'll be much easier to work steadily at one church than to substitute here and there as I've been doing these past weeks. When will I start?'

'At choir practice this coming Thursday night,' Mrs. Ludwig said. 'Can you make it?'

Sandy checked her calendar to make sure she had no other meetings scheduled on that night. 'Yes, I'll be there. And thank you for asking me.'

Mrs. Ludwig rose. 'The congregation is lucky to have you, Sandy, and I appreciate your decision. I'll report the good news to the committee immediately.'

After Mrs. Ludwig departed, Aunt Lotia came into the living room with Dave at her heels carrying a step ladder and a replacement bulb for the ceiling light in the hall.

'Congratulations,' Dave said. 'I've known this was in the air for some time. The whole choir has been hoping you'd say yes when Mrs. Ludwig called on you. It was all I could

106

do not to tip you off beforehand.'

Aunt Lotia sniffed.

'Your choir?' Sandy asked, searching Dave's face for an explanation. 'What do you mean by that? I thought you attended church in Janesville.'

Dave walked into the hall and set up the ladder, then he tucked his thumbs under his belt in his usual pose.

'I joined the local church last month. It's too far to drive to Janesville every Sunday, especially in the winter when the roads are likely to be slick.'

Aunt Lotia steadied the ladder as Dave prepared to change the light bulb. Sandy was glad Dave would be in the choir, but she sensed her aunt's disapproval even before she spoke.

'That makes three nights a week you'll be tied up,' Aunt Lotia said. 'Doesn't leave a young girl much time to enjoy herself, seems to me.'

'But I enjoy my work,' Sandy pointed out. 'I'm lucky to be able to do something I like. Just think of all the people who dread going to their jobs each day. I love almost every minute of my work. And you'll have to admit that the sketching class isn't work. That's strictly recreation.'

'That's not the point.' Aunt Lotia pulled her dress collar up under her chin. 'You're just doing too much. You'll have a breakdown if you don't let up.'

Sandy went to the desk and picked up paper and pencil. 'Sit down a minute, Aunt Lotia. I want to show you some figures. I can prove I'm not even working a forty-hour week.'

'I'll see you two later,' Dave said, folding the ladder. 'Good luck with the new job.'

'I'm not even working full time,' Sandy repeated to her aunt after Dave left them. 'I teach four hours each afternoon, Monday through Friday. That's twenty hours.'

'And you teach all morning Saturday and part of the afternoon,' Aunt Lotia said. 'Don't forget that. That's at least a total of twenty-six hours. Choir practice and the Sunday-morning service will require an average of another four hours or more, if you count your hours of individual practice time.'

'Okay.' Sandy nodded. 'Thirty-two hours. And the theory class will meet for two hours a week. That makes thirty-four hours. See? I'm not exactly overworked. And I had hoped to do better financially. I'm only earning around seven hundred dollars a month.'

'*Only?*'

'Maybe that sounds like good pay for a beginner,' Sandy said. 'But remember, I'll have three months when classes are dismissed and when the church choir is on vacation. Not all my private pupils will take summer lessons.' Sandy wanted to add that her earnings in Brunston didn't come close to matching the teaching salary she would have received in Chicago, but she didn't want to bring up that subject.

'But you don't have the living expenses here that you would have in a big city,' Aunt Lotia said as if reading Sandy's mind.

'That's true.' Sandy smiled to cover up her true feelings. Hadn't she given up adventure and independence for these practical living arrangements? 'I've put away a good bit of my earnings. We should be able to manage that surgery for you before too long.'

'I can't let you spend all your savings on me,' Aunt Lotia protested. 'I won't have it.'

'You can't keep me from doing it.' Sandy smiled again, but in her heart she still worried about whether her aunt could stand to undergo surgery. She really must talk to Dr. Ward about it before Aunt Lotia raised her hopes too high. Her heart condition might force her to change her plans.

Snow fell three times in the first days of December, and as Brunston's merchants began displaying yuletide decorations, Aunt Lotia began discussing family Christmas plans.

'Is everyone coming here again?' Sandy asked. 'Surely you should take it easy this Christmas. You've barely had time to rest up from your Thanksgiving entertaining!'

'Nonsense,' Aunt Lotia replied calmly. 'Christmas dinner is no more of a problem than any other dinner. And it's a tradition. Of course everyone's coming here. I wouldn't have it any other way.'

'I'll have to admit I'm glad,' Sandy said. 'Since I missed seeing everyone on Thanksgiving Day, I'm especially eager to see them this time. And I'll be here in person to help with the last-minute details.'

'We did hold a family council and decide to make it a buffet dinner,' Aunt Lotia told her. 'Everyone is going to bring something. I argued against it, but they insisted. Of course, we'll still do most of the fixing. You'll invite Bart, won't you?'

Sandy hesitated. Her Thanksgiving invitation to the Towners had been poorly received. And after all their differences, she didn't know whether Bart would even talk to her or not. Sandy sighed. What a way to enter the Christmas season! But how could she explain her feelings to Aunt Lotia?

'If you don't ask him, I will,' Aunt Lotia sniffed. 'And we'll ask his father, too. We always have plenty of room and plenty of food. Christmas must be a lonely time for those two. Go call Bart right now while we're speaking of it. Tell him to ask his father. Tell him I'm expecting them both.'

Sandy went to the telephone, not so much because her aunt insisted but because she herself wanted to get the deed finished. It was the practical thing to do. Bart could either say yes or no right now. She would not spend the Christmas season wondering about him, disturbed over his sulky moods and ill-concealed anger.

'Sorry, Sandy,' Bart said in response to her invitation. 'Dad's going skiing in Aspen with some business acquaintances, and I plan to have dinner at the club. Why don't you dine with me? There's plenty of time for me to get another reservation confirmed. The club is very elegant at Christmastime. You'd like it.'

'No, thanks, Bart.' Sandy's voice was curt, and she didn't much care. This time her decision was swift and final. Holidays were family times; she was not going to break that tradition again.

'You'll go out with me on New Year's Eve, won't you?' Bart asked. 'Dance at the club and all?'

'Yes,' Sandy replied. 'I'd like to go.'

'Then, of course, we still have a date for the eighteenth of January,' Bart reminded her. 'You haven't forgotten?'

'Of course not. I'll look forward to both occasions. I'm sorry you and your father can't be with us for Christmas dinner. We would have enjoyed having you.'

Sandy replaced the receiver and reported the conversation to her aunt.

'You're not very diplomatic with that boy, Sandy,' her aunt said, scowling and shaking her head. 'You could see our relatives and still go out to dinner with him. A meal at the club

111

wouldn't be anything like spending the whole day in Chicago.'

'On the other hand, Bart could meet our relatives and have dinner here,' Sandy retorted. 'He could try to please me by doing what I suggest just for once. I just don't understand Bart. He seems so lonely and aloof, yet when I try to include him in things that are important to me, he'll have none of it. He's built a wall between himself and the rest of the world. The only time he's interested in people is when they come into Towner's Mart to buy furniture.'

'He's to be pitied, Sandy,' Aunt Lotia said softly. 'He's to be pitied.'

'What's that supposed to mean?' Sandy demanded. 'I feel as if there's some big secret about Bart that everyone knows except me. Why should I or anyone else pity Bart Towner? He has everything. Looks. Charm. Money. He has a job of his own choosing and he's on his way up. I see no reason to pity him.'

'Sandy, it's not like you to get so upset. Let's forget our differences over Bart Towner for the moment. I have other plans to make. Tomorrow is my day to go into Des Moines to do my Christmas shopping. I plan to leave early and arrive there when the stores open. Is there anything I can get for you while I'm in the city?'

'Aunt Lotia! You're not going to make that trip all alone this year, are you? What does

Dr. Ward say? Have you discussed it with him? If you must go, I'll take a day off from teaching and go with you. I'll not interfere with your shopping, but I will relieve you of the strain of driving.'

Sandy might as well have been talking to the wall. Aunt Lotia was determined to live her life on her own terms with no interference from doctors or nieces. This trip to Des Moines was another Christmas tradition. Aunt Lotia always spent one day shopping in the city at Christmastime. No one had ever been allowed to go with her. And she always returned laden with gifts. Where she got the money for her shopping spree was also a secret. Sandy suspected that she hoarded it, penny by penny, all through the year. But she never knew for sure. All she knew was that her aunt did a good job of shopping, for they were never short on Christmas gifts.

Aunt Lotia departed for the trip as scheduled, but by nightfall snowflakes began to drift down and she still had not returned. When the wind began to howl under the eaves of the house, Sandy sought Dave's advice.

'I'm worried about her,' she confessed. 'Really worried. I knew she had no business driving those fifty miles alone, but I couldn't reason with her. It'll be my fault if anything's happened to her. I shouldn't have let her go.'

'You're her niece, not her keeper,' Dave said. 'Let's build a fire. That will give her a

113

warm welcome when she returns. And I'm sure she'll be here soon. Your aunt's not one to let a few snowflakes get her down.'

Sandy agreed with the fire-building idea, but Dave did most of the work. When he had some apple logs blazing, Sandy popped corn, and they sat around the fire and enjoyed their snack while they waited for the sound of Aunt Lotia's car in the driveway. The mingled fragrances of the fire, the popcorn, and Dave's turpentine and paint odor made Sandy drowsy.

'In a way I envy Aunt Lotia,' Sandy said with a yawn. 'She'll come in with all her shopping done. She'll have everything wrapped and under the tree while I'm still trying to decide what to give to the people on my list.'

Dave poked at the logs, then replaced the fire screen. 'I suppose it would be a problem to select the appropriate gift for Bart Towner, the man who has everything.'

'You could have gone all night without saying that,' Sandy said in mock anger, 'but he is one of my problems. And you're another one. Don't think you're not.'

'I choose gifts for people by thinking of sensory perceptions. It's sort of a game. It's fun, but it also accomplishes something.'

'How do you mean? How do you do it? Or is it a secret?'

'No secret. I think of one person at a time. I ask myself what that person likes to hear, see, taste, smell, and feel. From the answers to those questions, I usually come up with a gift idea. For example, my twin sisters like the taste of chocolate, so candy is always a good gift for them. They also like to listen to the Three Bops, so a record is another good gift. They aren't hard to please.'

'What a clever idea! Let me think. What does Bart like to taste? Pickled peaches. Some gift! What does he like to touch?' Sandy thought for a moment. 'Smooth things. Like the leather upholstery in his car. He's always running his fingers over that sleek black leather. And he likes the feel of silk. His ties are always made of silk, and his shirts have a soft, silky texture.'

Before Sandy could think of any more of Bart's favorite sensory perceptions, she and Dave heard Aunt Lotia's step on the porch. They had been so busy talking, they hadn't even heard the car in the driveway. Dave helped her in with her bundles, and Sandy hurried to the kitchen to make hot chocolate.

'No peeking, now,' Aunt Lotia warned as Dave arranged the packages in his arms. 'Take those bundles straight to my bedroom, please. I'll take care of them in private.'

As Sandy came back with the pot of hot chocolate and three mugs, a slip of paper fluttered to the floor from one of the bags Dave was carrying. Setting the pot and mugs on the coffee table, she stooped to retrieve the paper.

'Here,' Aunt Lotia said swiftly. 'Give that to me.' She grabbed the paper from Sandy's hand, but not before Sandy caught a glimpse of the words 'Goodwill Industries' printed across the top in bright blue letters.

Goodwill Industries! So that was how her aunt managed to buy so many gifts on her restricted budget! That was why she always insisted on going to Des Moines alone and kept her shopping trip such a secret! Sandy pretended not to have seen the writing on the slip of paper. She would not wound her aunt's pride by betraying that she shopped at a second-hand store.

Sandy thought about Christmases past. She had never once suspected that her gifts from Aunt Lotia weren't absolutely brand-new. But Aunt Lotia was talented with a needle and thread as well as with a paint brush. How she must have worked to make her Christmas gifts appealing! Sandy understood a lot of things now that she had never considered before.

During the next few days Sandy was so busy that she could hardly believe it when Christmas Day finally arrived. Although it was a long-awaited holiday, she was up before sunrise. She and Dave exchanged gifts before breakfast, before he left to spend the day with his family in Janesville.

Dave had given her an appointment book that he had made and decorated himself, and she gave him a double recipe of her caramel bars and another Brahms recording. The gifts in themselves were inexpensive, but the warmth they generated was priceless.

The Towner butler arrived in a limousine to bring Sandy her gift from Bart, and while Sandy was surprised, she had the presence of mind to send Bart's gift back with him. But somehow it was not a very satisfactory gift exchange. When the butler had departed, Sandy opened the package from Bart.

'A music box!' Aunt Lotia exclaimed. 'How grand! Sandy, you just don't know how lucky you are to have a nice young man like Bart.'

It was indeed a grand gift. Sandy was impressed. The gold exterior was studded with jewels, and when Sandy peeked inside the velvet-lined box, a brittle tune began to play. The metal of the box felt cold to her touch, and she set it on the back stairway as their guests began arriving at the front door.

The rooms soon became overheated with the number of people, and Sandy tried to open doors and windows to cool everyone off. But Aunt Addie complained of the draft and went around closing everything that Sandy had opened.

Aunt Cecile and Uncle Jake arrived, bringing Cousin Henrietta and her three children. Great-aunt Bessie and her three daughters and their husbands and children arrived in a caravan of three cars. Sandy's face flushed with pleasure as she visited with her relatives. But in the back of her mind she thought about Bart and the invitation that she had turned down. What was Bart doing? Where was he? Had he chosen another girl to share the holiday with him? If he was at the club, perhaps he was to be pitied as Aunt Lotia had said. A person belonged with a family on Christmas Day.

After the buffet dinner Sandy and her Aunt Addie volunteered to do the dishes. Sandy tried to keep her mind on Aunt Addie's account of a pre-Christmas shopping trip, but her thoughts kept slipping back to Bart. On Thanksgiving Day she had been unhappy with Bart, and now on Christmas Day she found that she was unhappy without him. What was wrong with her? How could her feelings be so unstable?

It was late that night after all the guests had departed when Sandy heard Dave's car in the driveway. Grabbing her coat, she hurried out to open the garage door for him. It wasn't a service she usually performed, but she needed to talk to someone, someone her own age.

'Have a good day?' Sandy asked as Dave slid from his old car.

'Great!' Dave replied. 'But I could use a little silence. What a family! Hey, look! It's beginning to snow. Let's walk around the block and listen to the snowflakes fall.'

Sandy fell in step with Dave, and they walked in comfortable silence. She felt the snowflakes like icy pinpricks against her cheeks, she tasted their nothingness on her tongue, and she heard her shoes squeaking underfoot. The whole world was a canvas of white, and its beauty held her speechless. When they returned to the house, Sandy still had no words when Dave leaned down and kissed her lightly on the cheek.

CHAPTER TEN

Sandy enjoyed the relaxed days of the Christmas vacation. She spent hours practicing on the piano and more hours practicing on the church organ.

Except for a brief call from Bart, thanking her for her Christmas gift, she heard nothing more from him, and she and Aunt Lotia and Dave spent many evenings around the fireplace playing Scrabble or Monopoly. On some evenings when they retired early, Sandy couldn't help wondering what she might have been doing had she taken the teaching job in Chicago.

On New Year's Eve Sandy worried about whether Bart would remember their date. He hadn't telephoned her for days. But he called for her at the exact time they had agreed on. Sandy wanted to go to the country club, yet she did not attach to it the importance that

Bart seemed to.

The clubhouse was a white frame mansion south of Brunston that stood at the end of a narrow lane, high on a hill overlooking the swimming pool and golf course. Tonight it was decorated to suit the occasion.

Plastic snowflakes dangled from the ceiling, a tall fir bedecked with tinsel and balls touched the rafters, and garlands of evergreen scented the whole house. A long-haired guitar group outfitted in tuxedoes and party hats provided music.

Tables and chairs ringed the dance floor. Sandy was inhaling the mingled fragrance of pine boughs and Chanel No. 5 when Bart spotted Dave in the crowd.

'Wonder who let him in?' Bart muttered. 'He's certainly not a member here.'

Sandy returned Dave's friendly wave and studied the pretty blonde girl at his side. 'He's probably just an interloper like myself, a guest of his date.'

Sandy was surprised at her reaction to seeing Dave at the club, and she was curious about his date. She hadn't known that he was seeing any local girl. Of course, she had little idea who his friends in Janesville were.

Bart scowled as he found an empty table and pulled a chair out for Sandy. Clearly, he was upset at seeing Dave at the clubhouse.

'Give me your coat,' he said. 'I'll hang it on the hall rack for you. It'll just be a bother to us here.'

Sandy obliged, and while Bart was away on his errand, Dave strolled over to where she sat alone. He was dressed in a dark, well-cut suit, and Sandy guessed that she could see her reflection in the shine on his shoes.

'Would you and Bart like to join Gloria and me?' Dave asked.

'Thanks a lot,' Sandy replied. 'I'll ask Bart when he returns. But who is she, this Gloria?'

'She's my cousin. I'm pinch-hitting for her boy friend who's in Vietnam. We'd like to have you join us. There's plenty of room at our table. You'll like Gloria; she's a swell girl. She's just here for the holidays.'

'Thanks a lot, but no, thanks,' Bart said, striding past Dave and seating himself across from Sandy. 'I heard the build-up, but we'd like to spend this evening alone, if you don't mind.'

'Suit yourself.' Dave smiled at Sandy and strolled back to where Gloria waited at their table.

'That was unkind,' Sandy said when Dave was out of earshot. 'Dave was just being friendly. He's here with a cousin of his. It wouldn't have hurt to have joined them for the evening. After all, this is supposed to be a celebration.'

'That guy's always being friendly,' Bart growled. 'Too friendly to suit me. What a creep! I don't know what you see in him.'

121

'I see a very nice guy.' Sandy frowned, then forced a smile. 'But please, let's don't fuss tonight. This is a time to be gay.'

'Agreed.' Bart covered her hand with his, and when a waitress came by, he ordered drinks for them. 'Shall we dance? I want to show you off. You'll be the talk of the club.'

Sandy followed Bart onto the dance floor, where he tried some fancy steps with intricate twirls while a vocalist sang a snappy number. Sandy followed his lead without faltering. But this group of people was unlike the crowd at the Roundtable. They took Bart in their stride. No one left the floor to make room for a Towner exhibition. In fact, so many more couples began to crowd the floor that Bart had to curtail his swoops and glides and conform to the more popular mode of dance used by the other people on the floor.

'May I cut in?'

Sandy looked up at the sound of Dave's voice. Color flared in Bart's cheeks, and his shoulder muscles tightened, but he let Dave dance with her.

'You're a good dancer, Dave,' Sandy said as they kept time to the music. 'You have an excellent sense of rhythm. You should dance more often.'

'I really feel quite ill at ease about it,' Dave admitted. 'But I just couldn't stand to let old Bart monopolize you all evening. How do you stand that creep?'

Sandy laughed. 'You two ought to form a mutual-admiration society. What did you do with Gloria?'

'She's dancing a set with her father while her mother repairs her make-up.'

Sandy and Dave danced the rest of that set, and when Dave took her back to Bart's table, she felt more relaxed than she had all evening. She wished Dave and Bart could be friends, but Bart's greeting was curt, and Dave melted off into the crowd without comment.

Bart was quiet and withdrawn for the rest of the evening. Even Aunt Lotia would have had to admit that he was sulking. Sandy was glad when midnight arrived and the group played 'Auld Lang Syne.' Bart had led her onto the dance floor and was pausing to give her a New Year's kiss when a group of young men came whooping through the room shouting and laughing, blowing noisemakers and ringing cowbells.

They made a wide circle around the room, and it seemed quite accidental that they stopped beside Bart. Before Sandy realized what was happening, one of the men pulled out a gun, aimed it at Bart, and pulled the trigger.

A loud explosion shook the room, black smoke rose in the air, and a small flag bearing the caption 'HAPPY NEW YEAR!' popped from the gun barrel.

A hush fell over the room as the smoke

drifted toward the ceiling. Like the rest of the crowd, Sandy was startled into silence at first. Then when she realized the joke, she laughed with the others.

But Bart did not laugh. Doubling his fist, he smashed it into the face of the practical joker with the gun, then swung at the man carrying the cowbells. It took three attendants to subdue Bart, and then he was so deathly pale that Sandy became frightened. Before she could speak, Bart strode from the room, leaving her standing alone on the dance floor.

'Need a friend?' Dave asked, appearing at her side. 'Come on. Let's go sit down.'

Sandy felt like a thermometer with all the red mercury running to her head as Dave guided her off the floor. How could Bart have behaved in such a disgraceful manner! Where had he gone? Had he forgotten about her? Sandy felt tears stinging her eyelids, and she swallowed hard, trying to control them.

'Come on,' Dave said. 'You need to get out of here. I'll get your coat and drive you home.'

'But what about your date?' Sandy mumbled. 'What about Gloria? She may not be ready to leave yet. I don't want to spoil anyone's evening.'

'Gloria's parents are on the planning committee,' Dave said. 'She's going to stick around and help them clean up after the dance. And it may go on for an hour or so longer. You're the one who needs an escort.'

Sandy felt numb as she let Dave help her into her coat. 'I don't know what could have come over Bart. He's never behaved like that before. I'm really worried about him. He was so pale.'

'Save your worrying,' Dave said. 'Bart'll be all right. He's tough. That was a mighty dirty trick to pull, especially on him, but he'll recover.'

'What do you mean, especially on him?' Sandy asked. 'I can't stand practical jokers, either. What do you mean?'

'Nothing. Nothing at all.' Dave eased a pathway through the crowd, and Sandy followed him outside.

On the drive home Dave and Sandy agreed not to mention the incident to Aunt Lotia.

'She'd only worry,' Dave said. 'She thinks the sun rises and sets in Bart Towner's pocket.'

'I'll just tell her the good things,' Sandy promised, but she wondered why there were usually unpleasant things to hide where Bart was concerned.

Sandy did not hear from Bart until three days after her teaching schedule had started again. His apology came in the form of a dozen roses, and Aunt Lotia was much more excited than Sandy as she displayed them in a silver pitcher in the living room. Sandy said nothing. Since she hadn't told her aunt of Bart's behavior on New Year's Eve, there was little she could say now. But she was not to be bought with a dozen roses. She refused to call Bart even to say thank you.

Several days later Aunt Lotia suggested inviting Bart to dinner.

'Let's not,' Sandy said. 'You've been entirely too busy lately, and I'm really much too tired to help prepare a company meal.'

'That's just the trouble,' Aunt Lotia said tersely. 'You're too tired or you're too busy. It's always something. You're too busy for your own good. Three nights a week you spend working. It's small wonder that Bart doesn't call you any more. You still have a date with him for the country-club dance, don't you?'

'I suppose so,' Sandy said, wishing that she could forget the date. 'At least he hasn't called to break it.'

As if by mutual agreement, neither Sandy nor her aunt mentioned Bart's name until the day of the dance. It was in the afternoon, shortly before her pupils were due to begin arriving, that the telephone rang.

'This is Miss Sandy Stafford speaking. Who is this, please?'

A strange voice flowed over the wire. 'This is Gertrude Hammond, Secretary of the Community Concert Association. We have a serious problem, and I hope you will be able to help us out.'

'I'll try,' Sandy said. 'What is it?'

'As you probably know, Florence Carol is scheduled to sing in Brunton tonight. Over a

126

thousand tickets have been sold. And now Miss Carol's pianist has a severe case of the flu and cannot perform. Miss Stafford, do you think you could accompany Florence Carol tonight?'

Sandy hesitated, thoughts of Bart uppermost in her mind. 'Couldn't you fly in a pianist from Chicago?'

'There are storm warnings,' Mrs. Hammond replied. 'I called the airport. All flights in and out of Chicago have been cancelled. Miss Carol is willing for you to substitute. We've given you a good recommendation.'

'When could we rehearse?' Sandy asked, finding her bearings. 'Is her music available?'

'Miss Carol could rehearse with you at four o'clock. If you could report at the performance hall immediately, I'll have the music ready for you. You could look it over and practice for an hour or so. You understand that Miss Carol must save her voice for the performance.'

'Of course. I understand. I'll meet you at the hall in fifteen minutes. I'll need that much time to rearrange my own teaching schedule.'

For a moment after the telephone conversation Sandy just stared into space. Then, at Aunt Lotia's request, she repeated the information she had just received. She, Sandy Stafford, was to accompany a Metropolitan opera star. In her wildest dreams Sandy had never visualized such an event. Florence Carol!

'But you have a date with Bart tonight,' Aunt Lotia said plaintively. 'You must call Gertrude Hammond back and cancel out. You must! Had you forgotten about Bart?'

Sandy looked at her aunt as if she were speaking a foreign language. 'Aunt Lotia! You don't expect me to put an ordinary date before Miss Carol's concert, do you? This woman is in big trouble. And I can help. As a musician my first responsibility is to her. Hundreds of people will be disappointed if she fails to appear in concert tonight.'

'But as a young woman who may someday marry and lead a normal family life, your first duty is to Bart Towner.' Aunt Lotia fussed and fumed and paced. 'I refuse to let you break that date for this Miss Watchamacallit!'

'You forbid me?' Sandy's voice was so quiet that she hardly recognized it as anger boiled up inside her. 'You can't forbid me, Aunt Lotia. I'm not a child. I'm an independent woman. I know what's right, and I'll make my own decisions. I'm sorry to upset you so, but I must give my time to Miss Carol.'

Aunt Lotia grew pale as paper, and she clutched at her chest with one hand. 'You'll be the death of me, Sandy. Me, your Aunt Lotia, who took you in when you had no one. Me, the one who has done so much for you.'

'What's going on in here?' Dave asked, just coming in from school. 'I could hear you two yelling clear out to the garage.'

Sandy breathed a sigh of relief as she saw Dave, but she couldn't match his light mood.

'Take care of Aunt Lotia, Dave. An emergency has come up. I must leave at once.'

Glancing at her watch, Sandy realized that it was too late to telephone her pupils to cancel her afternoon lessons, so she wrote a note and taped it to the door with her apologies and with suggestions for evening make-up lessons the following two nights after supper.

Sandy did not take her aunt's car since her aunt was so angry with her. The concert hall was only a few blocks away, and with a fast pace she could get there in just a few minutes. She tried not to think as she hurried along. If this was independence, it was hard won. And now she was dependent on Florence Carol. Perhaps independence was only the right to choose upon whom she would be dependent.

CHAPTER ELEVEN

The spotlight trained on the grand piano on center stage made the rest of the concert hall seem dark by comparison, and Sandy jumped in surprise as Mrs. Hammond stepped from the shadows near the rear entrance.

'Miss Stafford! Thank goodness you're here. I've been so worried. Nothing like this has ever happened to the Association before.' Mrs.

Hammond handed her a sheaf of music. 'Here are the numbers Florence Carol will perform tonight. I do hope you'll be able to manage. Oh, but I know you will—you must.'

Sandy felt Mrs. Hammond's doubts, but she was determined to appear confident. 'I'm sure everything will go well. I'll practice alone until Miss Carol arrives. Thank you so much for bringing the music.'

Mrs. Hammond turned to leave the hall, and Sandy hurried to the stage. Then she remembered Bart. Hurrying to the pay phone backstage, she tried to call him. The telephone rang for a long time before anyone answered, and when Bart's voice came over the line, Sandy blurted her news.

'I'm sorry, Bart. You must believe that. But this is a real emergency. I can't let Florence Carol down.'

'But you can let Bart Towner down,' he replied. 'That's clear enough.'

'Come to the concert, Bart. Use my ticket. You'll enjoy it. We'll go on to the dance afterward.' Sandy waited for Bart's reply, but suddenly she found herself listening to the dial tone. Bart had hung up.

Sandy stamped her foot in anger and dismay. But she had no time for a display of temper. She had to get busy; she had to put Bart from her mind.

Once seated on the piano bench, she uncovered the keyboard, sorted through the music, and laid the most difficult numbers out for immediate study and practice. She forced herself to concentrate on the task at hand.

Arias. Art songs. Selections from light opera. Sandy began sight-reading the aria accompaniments. Her fingers shook a bit, but she soon gained control. Gradually she trained herself to skip the easy passages and concentrate on the difficult measures. The art songs were relatively simple, but some of the German numbers required intense concentration.

Sandy didn't realize how long she had been working until a throaty voice interrupted her.

'Ah, you must relax for a bit, Miss Stafford. You work much too long and too hard. You will have nothing left to give tonight at the performance.'

'Miss Carol!' Sandy exclaimed, awed by the presence of the great singer. 'I didn't hear you come in.'

She sat as if in a trance as the tall, buxom woman took her place in the graceful curve of the grand piano. The overhead spotlight made her blonde chignon gleam like polished gold, and her regal air was evident as she sang two or three scales to warm up her voice.

'I see you can't relax,' Miss Carol said. 'And I understand. You are indeed put in a tight spot, and I am so sorry. It is most unfair to you.'

'I am only thinking of you,' Sandy said

truthfully. 'I know what a good pianist means to a performer. I'll—I'll do my best. What selection would you like to rehearse first?'

'The Wagner.' Miss Carol smiled. 'It will be first on the program. If I sing *sotto voce,* you will understand that I am conserving my voice.'

Sandy nodded, and at Miss Carol's signal she began the accompaniment. Time sped by. Number after number was laid aside. In general, the rehearsal went well. Miss Carol was patient when Sandy needed to repeat a passage or change a tempo. Her facial expression and her entire manner remained as pleasant as her voice throughout the practice session.

'You are a gem,' Miss Carol proclaimed after they had rehearsed the complete program. 'Just watch me for tempo changes and all will go smoothly. I don't know how I could be so lucky. So many pianists know nothing of accompanying. And in a smaller city like Brunston, I just didn't know what to expect.'

'Thank you, Miss Carol,' Sandy replied. 'If I may I'll take this music home with me. I will have a few more minutes to practice before concert time. There are still many passages that need more attention on my part.'

'Do you have a car?' Miss Carol asked.

Sandy shook her head. 'I'm sorry. But I'll be glad to telephone for a taxi for you. Brunston has excellent service.'

'No, no,' Miss Carol laughed. 'I was not concerned for myself. I have a limousine. My chauffeur will be glad to take you home and call for you before curtain time this evening.'

Sandy hated to be a burden to anyone. It damaged her image of herself as an independent person. But there was no arguing with Florence Carol. The black-uniformed chauffeur stopped the limousine in front of Aunt Lotia's house, and from the corner of her eye Sandy caught a movement at Grace Cantrell's window and another at the house across the street. This would give the neighborhood ladies something to talk about for a long time. She bid Miss Carol farewell and promised to be ready to return to the concert hall in two hours.

Dave met Sandy in the hallway, and from his expression she knew that there was trouble.

'I think your aunt is ill,' Dave said, speaking before Sandy could take her coat off or say a word. 'She's lying down, but she's moaning and groaning and calling for you. What on earth happened between you two?'

'Oh, Dave!' Sandy gulped. 'I shouldn't have run off like that. And you shouldn't have to face my problems. Why didn't you call me? Didn't Aunt Lotia tell you that I was at the concert hall?'

'She told me, but I decided not to call. She wouldn't let me telephone the doctor. She wanted none of that. I insisted on calling

Dr. Ward about three different times, but she wouldn't hear of it. I knew you two had argued, and I thought that if your aunt wasn't sick enough for the doctor, she wasn't sick enough to ruin your big chance—whatever that may be.'

'Big chance?' Sandy repeated. 'Oh, Dave! I'm just helping out tonight at the concert. I couldn't leave Florence Carol in a jam. But I may have to call someone in to stay with Aunt Lotia if she's really sick. Perhaps Grace Can—'

'You needn't be whispering in the hallway,' Aunt Lotia called to Sandy from the living room. 'I'm not sick, and come on in here where I can see you—both of you.'

Sandy looked at Dave and raised her eyebrows. 'She doesn't sound sick to me.'

'I felt all along that she was putting me on,' Dave said. 'Or else just having a temper tantrum like a little kid. I turn her over to you.' He headed upstairs to his apartment, and Sandy went inside to face her aunt alone.

'Before you say one word to me, let me apologize,' Aunt Lotia said, sitting up and putting a sofa pillow behind her back. 'I don't know what came over me. You know what you want to do with your life. I'll not interfere again. Perhaps you have no plans for marriage and family. But I do hope you let Bart down easy about tonight. It was such a long-standing date that I'm sure he was terribly upset.'

'Oh, Aunt Lotia!' Sandy hugged her aunt

134

and tried to put thoughts of Bart from her mind. 'I'm the one who should apologize for upsetting you so. And don't worry for one minute about Bart. I called him from the concert hall. He's probably already got another girl lined up for tonight's dance.'

'He has a flock of girls sitting around waiting for him to call,' Aunt Lotia said, nodding. 'I know. I hear all the local gossip. You have managed to snag yourself quite a catch, yet you don't even seem to know it or care.'

Sandy laughed. 'I really haven't been trying to snag anyone. I started to say that Bart and I are just good friends. But that's not true. Good friends don't fuss and argue as much as we do. I guess we're just sometimes friends, off-again, on-again friends. I hope I won't bother you if I practice for the next hour and a half or so. There are many passages I must smooth out before the performance tonight.'

'Of course you won't bother me.' Aunt Lotia got up and headed for the kitchen. 'I'll warm up some vegetable soup and bring you a cup when it's ready. That'll save you taking the time to come to the kitchen. Do you have some special clothes that you want me to get ready for you? I'd be glad to press or stitch something. I know you'll be rushed.'

Clothes! Sandy hadn't given a thought to what she would wear or how her hair should look. But it was too late to do anything fancy at this hour. She would just have to make do with whatever was at hand.

'I'll just wear my black velvet dress,' Sandy said. 'It will be neat and inconspicuous. All my floor-length dresses are too fussy. Anyway, a proper accompanist is supposed to remain in the background. I'm sure the audience will be so entranced with Florence Carol that they won't notice me or my clothes.'

Somehow Sandy lived through the harried hours until curtain time. She practiced. She gulped a cup of soup. Then she dressed.

Dave agreed to use Sandy's ticket and attend the concert. And he also agreed to accompany Aunt Lotia to the performance hall.

Window curtains fluttered all up and down the block as the chauffeured limousine called for Sandy. But this time Sandy barely noticed. Her mind was locked on fingering patterns and tempo markings.

Florence Carol was as relaxed as if she were singing in her own living room, and some of her self-confidence rubbed off on Sandy. Miss Carol held the audience spellbound as she displayed her multifaceted talents.

The concert progressed from beginning to end with a minimum of flaws. At the end of the program the applause was deafening, and the audience rose in a standing ovation as Miss Carol insisted that Sandy take her share of the bows.

After the curtain rang down for the last time, Mrs. Hammond appeared backstage and invited Florence Carol and Sandy to a reception at her home in Highland Terrace. Before she left the performance hall, she slipped an envelope into Sandy's hand.

'This is your pay. And along with it go the sincere thanks of the concert board. I don't know what we would have done without you tonight.'

Sandy's step was light as she followed Miss Carol outside. The air was sharp as a silver knife, and the stars hung so low that Sandy felt she could grab a few and scatter them like seeds. This time Sandy relaxed and enjoyed the luxury of a chauffeured car. How she wished she could share the pleasure with Dave and Aunt Lotia!

After Florence Carol directed the driver to the Highland Terrace address, she pressed something into Sandy's hand. In the dim light Sandy saw that it was a hundred-dollar bill.

'Miss Carol, I can't accept this! It's much too much! I'm just an amateur accompanist, and I was well paid by the concert board.'

'So this is a tip,' Florence Carol said. 'And I insist that you keep it. I would have been nothing without you tonight. Don't think that I don't know that.'

Then, leaning forward, Florence Carol spoke to her chauffeur. 'Pull over to the curb for a few minutes, Hawkins. Miss Stafford and

137

I need to talk a moment privately before we face the crowd at the reception.'

'But Mrs. Hammond . . . she'll be waiting for you.'

'She'll be waiting for *us*,' Florence Carol corrected. 'But waiting won't hurt anyone. There'll be food to distract her guests. Sandy, have you ever thought of going to New York? I mean going there to work as a professional musician?'

Suddenly Sandy found herself pouring out her story about Chicago, about her aunt's health, about her endeavors in Brunston as a professional musician. The only thing she omitted was her difficult time with Bart Towner, and she felt sure that Florence Carol wouldn't be interested in that.

Miss Carol listened quietly until Sandy finished speaking.

'From what I make of your story, I would say that you have made the correct decisions. Your place is in Brunston, at least for the time being.' Florence Carol smiled. 'I seldom encourage any aspiring musician to come to New York. The competition is unbelievable, but you are an exception. If you ever decide to leave Brunston and pursue your musical career in New York, I want you to call me. Call me collect from anywhere you happen to be. I will be happy to help you in any way I can, and to recommend you to the New York agencies as an accompanist. Of course, my recommendation will not insure you a job, but it will ease your path to success. Will you promise me to do that?'

'Of course,' Sandy said. 'You are very kind to make such a generous offer. But I really have no plans to go to New York City.'

Once she had Sandy's promise, Florence Carol ordered her chauffeur to drive on to the reception. In a matter of minutes they were surrounded by well-wishers and autograph-seekers.

Presently one group of ladies drew Sandy aside. She recognized two of them as members of her aunt's Wednesday Music Club.

'We want you to consider teaching a piano class for adult beginners,' a spokesman for the group said. 'We think there are a lot of ladies in Brunston who might be interested in piano lessons. Will you have time to meet with us and discuss the possibility?'

Sandy was in no mood to refuse anybody anything. By teaching an adult piano class, she would again be broadening the scope of her usefulness in Brunston. And she would be increasing her earning capacity. She tried not to think of her aunt's reaction to such a plan. Aunt Lotia already thought she was over-worked, but Sandy felt certain she could persuade her to accept the idea. After all, this would be daytime work. It was the many evening hours spent in working that her aunt seemed to object to.

'Of course we can discuss it,' Sandy said. 'It sounds like a fine idea to me. Would you like to come to my studio tomorrow morning about ten o'clock? We could talk about it then at length.'

CHAPTER TWELVE

The idea of teaching piano lessons to adults snowballed beyond Sandy's wildest expectations. By early spring she had a full morning schedule for four days a week.

Aunt Lotia fussed and argued that Sandy was doing far too much, but Sandy felt that at last she was working to capacity. She experienced a new sense of independence, and as her work load grew, so did her income.

On one of Sandy's free mornings she was helping Aunt Lotia arrange lilacs in a vase when she brought up the subject of her aunt's surgery.

'I have enough money saved now to make a partial payment on the operation. With that and your medical and surgical insurance, we should be able to manage financially. You do want to go through with the surgery, don't you?'

'Of course I want to.' Aunt Lotia snipped a lilac stem. 'At first I was reluctant. Nobody likes the idea of being confined to a hospital bed. And I suppose everyone seeks an easier way out. I know I did. I thought perhaps I'd find some ointment or lotion that would diminish my disfiguration. But I realize now that Dr. Ward is right. The only way to get rid of these scars is to have them removed completely and thoroughly by surgery. I'll always be indebted to you for helping provide the means, Sandy. Always.'

'I don't want you to feel indebted at all,' Sandy said. 'I want to help. This is just one small opportunity for me to begin repaying some of your many kindnesses.'

'You are indeed a thoughtful niece.' Aunt Lotia stood back to admire her lilac arrangement.

'Why don't you see Dr. Ward about the operation?' Sandy suggested as she picked up the garden shears and lilac stems. 'I know you've mentioned it to him before, but I think it's time to talk over all aspects of the surgery.'

'I'll do that,' Aunt Lotia said. 'I've been putting it off. Guess I just needed someone to prod me a bit. I'm sure Dr. Ward will recommend a specialist. And there'll probably be a long wait and a lot of details to take care of. I'll make an appointment today. Dr. Ward's so busy he'll probably not be able to see me for a week or so.'

Sandy nodded. That would work out with her own plans. Her spring recital was scheduled for Friday night, and as soon as that

141

was off her mind, she wanted to visit with Dr. Ward personally. She wanted to know exactly what her aunt's chances were of having a successful operation. Was it practical for a heart patient to undergo surgery for cosmetic reasons? The question had been bothering her for months.

That evening Sandy was waiting for Bart to call for her. It would be the first time they had been out together for over a week. As she waited she made a list of pupils who were to appear in her recital. The list should go to the newspaper first thing in the morning.

Working from the list, Sandy noted the composition each child would perform as well as its composer, then she roughed out a program to present to the printer. She was so intent on her work that she didn't hear Dave enter the room until he spoke.

'Sandy, I have an idea that I hope you'll consider. It concerns your recital. You may not like it, but I'm hoping you'll listen.'

'Of course I'll listen.' Sandy laid her list aside. 'You sound so serious. What's up?'

'I wish you would consider adding some art work to your recital Friday night.' Dave sat down on a footstool across the room from Sandy. His eyes searched her face as he waited for her reaction.

'Art with a piano recital?' Sandy said. 'How would it work? What do you have in mind?'

'I'd like your permission to display an art

exhibit on stage, sort of as a background for the piano.' Dave stood and began to pace. 'This exhibit would include work done by pupils in my evening class. Their work gets little attention, although it's good. Such a display would give these people some public acclaim, and at the same time it would give your recital a unique setting.'

'Dave, it sounds fine to me. That stage always looks so bare, and the kids seem so lost as they walk across that vast expanse to the piano. Aunt Lotia and I try to fill it in with baskets of flowers, but I had never thought of adding an art exhibit. That is a unique idea.'

'I was hoping you'd agree with me. There's one other thing that you might be interested in.' Dave paused a moment. 'I have two ninth-grade pupils at school who like to paint to music. You know, they turn on a record and do an abstract painting that to them represents the sounds they are hearing. If you have a couple of pupils who are performing long numbers, my paint-to-music students might be able to give an onstage performance. Of course, they would be strictly in the background. I wouldn't want them to upstage the musicians.'

Before Sandy had time to think over the idea, the doorbell rang, and Aunt Lotia ushered Bart into the living room. When he saw Dave his face flushed, and he adjusted his gold tie as he and Dave nodded curtly to each other. Sandy covered the awkwardness of the moment with her enthusiasm.

'Bart! Hi! I'll be ready to go just as soon as I get my coat on. Dave's been telling me a grand new plan for making Friday night's recital more functional and interesting.'

Sandy repeated what Dave had just suggested to her and asked Bart's opinion as she hurried to the hall closet to get her coat.

Again Bart's hand automatically straightened his necktie before he spoke. 'I think it's a rotten idea.' He scowled. 'Whoever heard of a combination art exhibit and piano recital?'

'I have,' Sandy retorted. 'Just a few minutes ago. And I think it's a good idea. I thought you would agree.'

'Sandy, can't you see that this guy's just trying to horn in on your success? He's trying for a free ride on your professional reputation. And to have students painting by music—you'll be laughed out of Brunston! You can't be serious about considering such a thing.'

Sandy saw Dave's face flush, and he suddenly seemed as vulnerable as one of her students. She fought a desire to go to him and console him. How dare Bart be so needlessly cruel!

'I am very serious about using Dave's idea.' Sandy took three deep breaths and held her chin high. 'In fact, I'm preparing a publicity release for the Brunston *News*. Dave, will you

144

give me the names of your students? I'll see that they are mentioned in the pre-recital publicity.'

Bart scowled again. 'Since you seem to be so busy, we'll just forget about our date for tonight. I wouldn't want to stand in the way of your career.' Bart straightened his tie for the third time, then stalked into the hallway and slammed the front door behind him.

Aunt Lotia followed Bart to the porch, wringing her hands and apologizing for things that required no apology. Then Sandy heard her go to her room and close the door with a touch so firm that it was almost a slam.

'I'm sorry,' Dave said. 'I've upset everyone with this crazy scheme. Let's just forget the whole thing—forget I ever mentioned it. After all, Towner's Mart has a stake in your recital. They furnish the piano. You should do as Bart wishes, if only for business reasons. I don't want to cause any trouble between you two.'

'We certainly won't just forget the whole thing.' Sandy ran her fingers through her hair. 'We certainly won't! I think your art-display idea is good. The music and the paintings will enhance each other. I'm sure Bart's father would agree with me, and he's the one who owns that business.'

'But Bart is the manager,' Dave pointed out. 'Loaning you the piano is his idea.'

'I will not let Bart Towner tell me what to do. He's not thinking about the pupils or the recital, he's just thinking that he doesn't much like you personally. It's unfair to let personalities enter into this. I won't have it.'

Sandy paced back and forth for a few moments, and when she looked at Dave again, he was watching her with a strange expression.

'What's the matter?' Sandy asked. 'You haven't changed your mind, have you? I won't let you back out. You came to me with a good idea, and we'll use it. Why are you looking at me that way?'

Dave smiled. 'Guess I was just empathizing with you. It must be tough to be in love with such a difficult person as Bart Towner.'

Before Sandy could deny the words or splutter an answer, Dave had dashed up the stairs.

In love with Bart? Was she? How could she know for sure? If she was in love with Bart, why did she go against his wishes? If she wasn't in love with him, why did she let him make her so miserable?

Sandy was determined to use Dave's idea. And she was miserable. She refused to apologize to Bart. What did she have to apologize for? He was the one who should apologize to her for walking out on a date.

But in the days that followed, Bart didn't call her to make amends. On top of their rift, everything about the recital seemed to go wrong. Two of Sandy's best pupils had come down with chicken pox, and another good student had fallen and broken three fingers and sprained her wrist.

But in spite of everything, the recital came off as scheduled. The audience was much larger than usual, a fact which Sandy attributed to Dave's outstanding art exhibit. Dave looked especially handsome in an olive green suit and tie that matched his eyes, and as they stood together in a reception line after the performance, people were highly complimentary about the evening. The idea of combining art and music was well received.

'Guess we were a big success,' Dave said after everyone had left and they were alone in the recital hall. 'Like to go celebrate at the malt shop?'

'Love to,' Sandy replied, closing the piano and switching off some of the stage lights. 'I suppose the janitor will turn off the houselights and lock the doors.'

Dave's old car rattled as they drove through the soft spring evening, but Sandy didn't notice. She was still in a post-recital whirl. The malt shop was about to close, but the manager agreed to serve them if they would take the two chocolate malts someone else had ordered before walking out.

'It's okay with me.' Sandy sniffed the sweet fragrance of ice cream and syrup that permeated the shop. 'Chocolate is my favorite. You know that.'

Dave sighed. 'Sometimes I'm sure you must just go out with me for comic relief.' He grinned. 'The last time I took you here, we were almost run down by a car, and now we get leftover malts someone else ordered. It must be pure thrill for a gal who's used to convertibles and sophisticated evenings on the town.'

Sandy laughed, yet Dave's words had a sobering effect on her. Go out with Dave? She had never considered any of their get-togethers honest-to-goodness dates. They were just thrown together by circumstance— art class, choir practice, living in the same house. Yet she always had more fun with Dave on their impromptu meetings than she ever had with Bart. Dave never pouted and sulked or made demands on her time. He was just Dave, steady, even-tempered, and pleasant— and slightly Bohemian.

Their stay at the malt shop was short, and Sandy hated to see it end. When they arrived home, Aunt Lotia was waiting up for Sandy. She made polite conversation with Dave, but it was unlike her to wait up, and Sandy knew she had something important to say when they were alone.

'Bart's coming for dinner tomorrow night,' Aunt Lotia whispered when Dave had climbed the stairs to his apartment. 'I was afraid you two would never get back together if someone didn't help out a bit, so I called him this afternoon and invited him. It's really silly of you to be so aloof where Bart is concerned.'

'Oh, Aunt Lotia, I don't know what to say. Bart's so . . .'

'You'll never find a better boy than Bart,' Aunt Lotia declared. 'You do like him, don't you?'

Sandy sighed and stalled for time while she hung up her coat. But when she turned around, her aunt was still waiting for an answer.

'Of course I like him, but—'

'Then be on your best behavior tomorrow night.' Aunt Lotia wagged a forefinger at Sandy. 'Bart's sensitive. That makes him hard to get along with at times, but he's a good boy. And the two of you make a handsome couple. Heads turn, and people stare in admiration wherever you go.'

There was no use arguing with Aunt Lotia, and Sandy didn't really want to argue. She hated for Bart to think that she had instigated the invitation, but she did miss him. She missed him terribly, and she vowed to behave with more understanding toward him in the future. Maybe their arguments and misunderstandings were as much her fault as his. It was hard for her to give in, and it was even harder for her to apologize.

Sandy taught all morning on Saturday, then helped her aunt tidy the house and prepare dinner. It was good to keep busy; it kept her from worrying about meeting Bart again.

Bart arrived promptly at six-thirty, and Aunt Lotia had prepared all his favorite foods. The dinner was a great success. Everyone talked and laughed as if there had never been any rift at all.

'Even cherry pie!' Bart exclaimed as Sandy served the dessert. 'Miss Stafford, you are a marvel. You are surely the best cook in Brunston. If you ever entered your pies at the county fair, no one else would stand a chance of winning a blue ribbon!'

Sandy watched her aunt blush in pleasure as she passed Bart more cream for his coffee.

'It's a delight to cook for someone who enjoys it so,' Aunt Lotia replied.

The three of them chatted for a while after their meal, and before Aunt Lotia had a chance to pretend to be tired, Bart asked Sandy to go for a ride.

'It's a beautiful night,' he said. 'The top's down on the convertible, and we'll go count the stars. I hear that there are more to be seen in the springtime than at any other season.'

'Don't miss any,' Aunt Lotia said with a smile. 'It's been so nice having you with us this evening, Bart. You must come back more often.'

Sandy and Bart drove off, and then Bart turned into a road that led away from town. He drove slowly, and Sandy enjoyed the scent of spring that floated on the night air.

Making the turn into the lane that led to Half Moon Lake, Bart drove even more slowly, then he parked the car where they could see the moon and trees reflected on the surface of the water. They sat in silence for a few minutes, and when Bart spoke, there was a new, demanding urgency in his voice.

'Will you marry me, Sandy? Will you? You must know that I love you.'

Sandy felt her heart pound. Surely Bart could hear it. She was unprepared for such a question, totally unprepared. One minute Bart was angry with her, the next he was proposing marriage.

'Bart, you know I think a lot of you, but I had no idea how you felt. Let me think this over. I know you don't want a snap decision.'

'Right. I want you to think it over.' Bart settled down into the car seat. 'I want you to think it over carefully. And I want your decision to be yes. I can give you everything, Sandy. You can forget all those hours of piano lessons. We'll move to Chicago. We'll get away from this small-town atmosphere. I've done my groundwork here at the store, and Dad's ready to transfer me anywhere I want to go. All I have to do is to name the place. I know you wanted to go to Chicago very badly last fall.'

Sandy was too mixed up to reply. Months ago she might have leaped at the chance to go to Chicago. But that was because she had a job there, a job that promised independence. But now? How did she feel about Chicago now?

The silence of the lake and the woods grew heavy, and suddenly Sandy saw a shooting star. She watched it disappear and wondered if her chances for independence might not disappear in just such a manner if she married Bart. What would life with Bart Towner be like? Did she really love him?

'I have money, Sandy,' Bart said, breaking into her thoughts. 'And enough money can buy anything. I can get you in as an instructor in a private school, if that's what you'd like. Or you might even do a concert series on a limited basis. It might be a good way to introduce the Towner name in Chicago society. What do you say?'

'I need time to think about it, Bart.' Sandy wondered if Bart was thinking about her happiness or the Towner name. And was she thinking of his happiness and well-being or merely of her own independence? Just what did she and Bart want from life? 'You won't rush me into a decision, will you?'

Bart kissed her gently. 'No, I won't rush you into a decision. But I want you to discuss this with no one. Do you understand? No one. Not even your Aunt Lotia. I won't be publicly rejected, and I won't be the butt of more gossip.'

'I won't mention it to a soul,' Sandy promised. 'And when I make my decision, you'll know that it will be mine alone.'

CHAPTER THIRTEEN

Sandy slept fitfully that night, and each time she awakened, she seemed to hear Bart's voice coming from a great distance. The next morning her mind was still in such a turmoil over Bart's unexpected proposal that she missed three organ cues in the church service. She felt Dave's questioning gaze on her and tried not to look at the choir.

Was she in love with Bart? Could they ever make a go of marriage when they were so frequently at odds over trivial matters? Sandy wished she had the answers to her questions. Perhaps Bart would be easier to please, less demanding, once he was sure of her affections. Or perhaps the very fact that she had so many doubts was an answer in itself.

After church, as the choir members hung their robes in the music room, Dave approached Sandy with a twinkle in his eye and a grin on his face.

'Care to join me in the cemetery this afternoon?' he asked. 'It's a lovely day for hunting grave markers, and I think you need a break from your usual routine.'

When she realized that Dave wasn't joking, Sandy asked, 'Why are you hunting for grave markers? I can think of many more pleasant ways to break a routine as well as how to spend a Sunday afternoon.'

'I'm going to sacrifice the afternoon for art's sake.' Dave assumed a dramatic pose, chin up, hand over heart. 'Seriously, I have a lonesome job to do, and I'd enjoy some company. I'm going tombstone rubbing at the local cemetery. I'm planning a bulletin-board display of unusual art forms, and I want to show some of the art work that can be found on ancient grave markers. How about it? Want to come along with me? It might be a once-in-a-lifetime event.'

'Count me in. Nothing I'd rather do on a pleasant Sunday afternoon than go tombstone rubbing with the local art instructor. What time shall I be ready?'

'Right after lunch. Your aunt invited me to eat with her today. I think she sort of had the idea that you would be out with Bart, but I thought I'd ask you, anyway—just in case you and Bart had one of your spats. Hope you don't mind if your lunch twosome turns into a threesome.'

Dave had not asked anything about Bart, and Sandy made no comment on his statement. It was none of his concern when she went out with Bart. Yet she was surprised to find that she was eager to spend the afternoon with Dave. Should an engaged-to-be-engaged girl feel this way?

Aunt Lotia had prepared a simple salad lunch, and if Sandy's presence at the table surprised her, she didn't let on. As soon as they had eaten, Sandy and Dave left for the cemetery. Dave tried to persuade Aunt Lotia to accompany them, but she declined with a wry smile.

'Sounds unbelievable,' she said. 'Whatever is the world coming to?'

'She probably thinks you're really up to something,' Sandy said with a laugh as they got into the car. 'Whoever heard of tombstone rubbing? Certainly not I. And certainly not Aunt Lotia.'

'Before the afternoon ends, you'll be well versed on the subject,' Dave promised. 'When we get home you can explain it to her. You can even show her evidence of your activity.'

Dave kept his word. He parked his car in the oldest part of the cemetery, and after they had walked around a few minutes, he was pointing out grave markers that dated back to the nineteenth century.

'I had no idea that Brunston was such an old community!' Sandy gasped. 'Some of these markers are so worn that I can hardly read the inscriptions.'

'That's why I do rubbings.' Dave sat down on the grass and motioned Sandy to join him. He untied a folder of art supplies.

'First I tape this thin paper over the face of the grave marker, then I take a crayon and rub it across the paper. Like this.' Dave demonstrated the rubbing technique, and as

155

Sandy watched him work, words and dates appeared on the art paper as if by magic.

'I used to put a penny under a piece of paper and do that sort of thing,' Sandy said. 'Look! There's an angel in the upper corner. Oh! And look there, at the bottom of the page. It's a little lamb. I didn't see that at all when I was looking at the marker itself.'

'Some of these old stones were really works of art.' Dave removed the paper from the tombstone and filed it in his folder before walking on to a new site.

'How strange that we should find beauty in someone else's sorrow. It makes me feel guilty and sad.' Sandy swallowed around a wedge in her throat and began to wander through the burial grounds while Dave began rubbing another marker.

Only when she reached the newer part of the cemetery did she realize how far she had walked. She was just turning to go back to Dave when a low marker caught her eye. She read the inscription over and over again as if in a trance. When at last she looked up, Dave was at her side. Together they studied the words cut into the stone.

'Could it be?' Sandy whispered more to herself than to Dave. 'It must be. But I don't understand. The large marker bears the inscription "Susan Barton Towner." And look at the dates. Surely that must be Bart's mother's grave.'

'I understood that Mrs. Towner lived in Brunston all her life,' Dave said. 'What is so unusual about her being buried here?'

'Nothing,' Sandy said. 'Nothing at all. It's this other marker that really surprises me. This small brass one. Who was David Carlfred Towner? He was just a boy when he died. Look at those dates. David Towner couldn't have been Susan Towner's husband. Mr. Towner's still living. David must have been her son. Can that be possible?'

'Of course he was her son.' Dave looked puzzled, almost frightened. 'Didn't you know?'

'No.' Sandy's lips felt stiff, and her mouth was cotton dry. 'Bart never mentioned having a brother. Not in all the time we've been seeing each other has he ever mentioned such a thing. I guess I just took it for granted that he was an only child.'

Sandy pulled a pencil and a scrap of paper from her purse and jotted down the name and dates on the brass grave marker.

'I'm through working for today,' Dave said. 'Are you ready to go home?'

'Of course.' Sandy headed toward the hillside where Dave had parked the car. 'Let's go. I didn't know a cemetery could be so depressing.'

Sandy was glad when they got home, and she went straight to her room. Why had she gone with Dave on such a silly chase? She vowed to forget what she had seen. But she couldn't wipe the image of the Towner grave marker from her mind.

Sleep eluded Sandy most of that night, and the next morning before her lessons started, she made an excuse to Aunt Lotia to go downtown on an errand.

After parking the car, Sandy dashed into the public library and asked the librarian to see a file of old newspapers. She quoted the year from the Towner child's grave marker, the date that she had jotted down the day before.

'Most of our old papers are on film,' the librarian said. 'Do you have an exact date in mind? Not just the year, but the month and day?'

Sandy quoted the complete date of death that had appeared on David Carlfred Towner's tombstone. The librarian jotted it down, then excused herself. In a few moments she returned and motioned Sandy into a small booth. After demonstrating how to use the film, she left Sandy alone and went about her work.

The viewing booth was hot and stuffy, and it smelled of stale cigar smoke. Sandy felt perspiration bead on her upper lip as she saw the headlines from ten years ago.

'TOWNER BROTHERS INVOLVED IN ACCIDENTAL SHOOTING,' blared the terrible news, and Sandy read on.

'David Carlfred Towner died early this

morning from a gunshot wound accidentally inflicted by his older brother, Barton Towner. The boys had been out pheasant hunting and were returning home when Barton Towner's gun accidentally went off as he and his brother were crawling under a barbed-wire fence.'

Sandy didn't know how long she had been sitting in a trance in the stuffy viewing booth before the librarian returned to check on her. 'May I be of more assistance?' she asked. 'Is there something special I can help you find?'

'No. No, thank you.' Sandy forced what she hoped was a smile, but she felt as if her face were a mask that might crack at any moment. 'You were very good to go to so much trouble for me. I appreciate it.'

'It's a regular library service, miss,' the librarian replied. 'Come in any time. We are always glad to be of service.'

Somehow Sandy got home and existed through the rest of the day. Her body went through the motions of teaching, but her mind was far from her music lessons.

She felt as if she had just found the missing pieces to a broken plate. For the first time she could see the whole design clearly, but she wasn't sure that she could glue the pieces in their right places without the seams showing. What was she to do now that she knew Bart's secret?

Bart Towner had killed his brother. This was the mystery in Bart's past that Aunt Lotia had hinted at. This was why Dave had said that Bart had had a rough childhood. This was why Aunt Lotia felt so sorry for Bart and why she babied and humored him so. Everyone had known the secret but Sandy Stafford, the one person who really needed to know. And now that she knew, Bart's occasional strange behavior began to make sense to her.

No wonder Bart felt that Brunston was a town full of gossips. Even a child can tell when a town is talking about him, speculating, guessing. No wonder Bart felt an exaggerated need to be first, to appear in the best possible light at all times. What a terrible thing he had bottled inside himself for ten long years.

Sandy remembered the horrible scene at the New Year's dance. The explosion. The gun. Now she understood why Bart had reacted so violently. No wonder he avoided explanations. And maybe the tragedy in his life was in a way responsible for his dislike of Dave. The very name must surely remind Bart of his brother.

After supper that night Sandy made an excuse to drive to the post office. For a moment she thought Aunt Lotia was going to suggest that she go along just for the ride, but at the last minute Grace Cantrell dropped in. Sandy seized the opportunity to escape.

From the pay phone at the post office, Sandy called Bart and asked him to meet her.

Although only minutes passed, it seemed like hours before Bart arrived.

'Since when do we have to start meeting at the post office?' Bart asked as Sandy slid into his convertible almost before it stopped at the curb. 'Or were you stranded here and in need of a ride home? I expect that jalopy of your aunt's to die on you at any moment.'

'I had to talk to you, Bart,' Sandy said. 'Privately. I didn't want Aunt Lotia to hear, and you know she just accidentally happens to be where she can hear most conversations that take place at the house.'

Sandy paused, then, before she could change her mind, she plunged into the subject that had been worrying her.

'Why didn't you ever tell me that you had a younger brother? Why didn't you tell me about the accident? Why, Bart? Why? I just don't understand you. I've asked myself why a thousand times since yesterday, but I can't come up with a reasonable answer.'

'It's simple.' Bart met Sandy's gaze without faltering. He didn't even hesitate long enough to straighten his tie. 'I didn't tell you because I didn't want you to know. I wanted you to think that I was just a normal human being like anyone else. I knew the people in this town gossiped, but I was fairly sure that they wouldn't tell Bart Towner's girl that her boy friend was a murderer.'

'Murderer!' Sandy could hardly bear to say

161

the word, yet it slipped out.

'I figured people would probably assume that you already knew the worst. And I felt reasonably sure that your aunt wouldn't discuss it with you. She's done her best for me ever since I was a kid, and I have a strong feeling that she would like to see us together permanently.'

'Murderer.' Sandy whispered the word. 'How can you say that! Your brother's death was an accident. I read about it from a film of the newspaper at the library. An accident. There was not the slightest hint of murder.'

'Accident, murder, what's the difference?' Bart's knuckles grew white as he gripped the steering wheel. 'Dave's dead, and his death killed Mom. I'm really a double murderer. Under the circumstances, I suppose it was very unfair of me to ask you to marry me. But the world's an unfair place.'

Sandy was silent for a long time. The street lights flashed on. People came and went from the post office. But there was no sound in the car except Bart's heavy breathing. At last Sandy found words that she thought might help Bart.

'Have you ever heard of forgiveness, Bart? The people of this town have forgiven you your carelessness, whether you realize it or not. They try to be friendly, but you won't let them.

'Doesn't your store do more business than

any of the other furniture stores in town? Do you think people would patronize you if they thought you unworthy? Think about it, Bart. It's important to you. To us. Brunston has forgiven you, but you still have to forgive yourself. No one can do that for you.'

'I'm getting out of this town,' Bart said doggedly. 'I've told you that, and I mean it. The only way I can escape from my past is to leave it here behind me. To get out. I've asked you to come with me. The choice is yours.'

'You can't run away from yourself,' Sandy said almost pleadingly. 'It won't work. And you can't be a loner forever. People need people. I do. You do, too, whether or not you'll admit it. We all need each other in order to survive.'

'I don't need anyone but you. I can close the rest of the world out and forget the past when you're with me.'

'I have a wonderful idea,' Sandy said, ignoring Bart's words and the touch of his hand over hers. 'Let's join the Brunston society. Oh, I don't mean let's be socialites, I just mean let's be friendly to the people you know. Everywhere we've ever gone, couples have been friendly. They've asked us to join them. But you've built an invisible barrier between yourself and the world. I'll help you tear it down, Bart. Let's have a party. Aunt Lotia will give us a party to announce our engagement. Nothing would please her more. We'll invite all your old friends. We'll start an

163

exciting new life right here in Brunston.'

'No deal,' Bart said curtly. 'I wouldn't consider such a thing. A party! Friends! I don't have any friends. I just have acquaintances who whisper "murderer" behind my back. We'll go it alone. My way.'

Again Sandy hesitated a long time before replying, and when she spoke, it was with the conviction that she had lacked in her relationship with Bart all along.

'I can't marry you, Bart. I thought for a while that I loved you, and perhaps I do. But I can't live your kind of life. Whatever it is that I feel for you would soon wither and die.'

'Nor can I live your kind of life,' Bart countered. 'It's as simple and as awful as that.'

Before Bart could stop her, Sandy slid from the convertible and ran toward her aunt's car. When people turned to stare, she forced herself to walk. And on the drive home tears blurred her vision for several blocks, but she was composed by the time she greeted her aunt in their living room and broke the news to her.

'Aunt Lotia, Bart and I have broken up. This time it's for good. I'm sorry, but I thought you would want to know.'

'Oh, now, now,' Aunt Lotia began. 'True love never runs smooth. It's a cliche, but it's true. You've just had another quarrel. You'll make up. You always have. Things will seem brighter in the morning. You get a good night's

164

sleep and see if I'm not right.'

'But this time is different. You could have saved me a lot of heartache if you had told me about Bart's brother right from the start. His death is the key to Bart's whole personality.'

Aunt Lotia became so pale that the scars on her face turned a dark red, but she listened as Sandy told her about her visit to the cemetery, her trip to the library, her talk with Bart.

'You're breaking up with Bart just because he won't let you have a big fancy engagement party!' Aunt Lotia flared. 'I don't understand you, Sandy. You've gone daft.'

'No,' Sandy said. 'You don't understand. My desire that we have a party goes deeper than that. All these past few months I've tried to include Bart in my life. I really tried. Remember Thanksgiving? Christmas? But Bart wanted no part of our family at all. He wouldn't join any activities to please me. He wouldn't even go to Florence Carol's concert when I was playing. He would do nothing that would entail associating with other people.

'Aunt Lotia, any adventure that separates me from other people is the wrong adventure. I'm sure of it. I've never been so sure of anything in my whole life. A lifetime with Bart Towner would be meaningless—a mistake from the very start. *That's* why we've broken up.'

Aunt Lotia spluttered and snorted, but Sandy didn't give in to her arguments. She

165

merely left the room and climbed the stairs as if she hadn't heard a word her aunt had said.

CHAPTER FOURTEEN

For the next few weeks Sandy felt bereft. Bart's absence left a large gap in her life. She saw more and more of Dave, but in moments of weakness she was tempted to call Bart. She knew his pride would never allow him to call her again. But she fought the impulse. Calling him would do no good. Bart could no more adjust to her lifestyle than she to his. They were much better off apart.

Sandy reflected on her predicament. Men were lucky. When they broke up with a girl, all they had to do was call the next name on their list. But a girl could hardly do that, not even in this day of liberated women.

Sandy couldn't wear a sign around her neck proclaiming the end of her relationship with Bart, and so she was thankful for Dave. He helped fill the blank spaces in her life, and he was even-tempered and easy to be with. Sandy often smiled when she thought about it. Weren't artists supposed to be the temperamental ones?

One night as she and Dave walked home from sketching class, Dave stopped in front of an empty store.

'Look at this building. How I wish I could afford to rent it!' Dave pressed his forehead against the plate-glass window and peered inside the building like an urchin studying a bakery display.

Sandy gave Dave a sideways glance. 'Thinking of opening an art store downtown when so many of the merchants are moving out to the shopping center on the south side?'

'I'm not thinking of opening a shop,' Dave said. 'But I'd like to rent a place like this for an art studio. Just look at the space in there. I can hardly stand to see it going to waste like this.'

'It would make a neat studio at that,' Sandy agreed, mentally picturing the possibilities that the store offered. 'It would catch the north light, too. You could display your paintings and maybe make a few sales. Have you inquired about the price?'

Dave nodded. 'I could never afford it as a part-time venture. We might split the fee, though. Have you ever thought of moving your own private studio away from your aunt's house? It would give you more privacy at home as well as at work.'

'I've thought about it, yes,' Sandy admitted. 'But I can't disappoint Aunt Lotia. She likes my solarium studio. And when I'm there at the house I can keep an eye on her. I never know . . . I really have everything I need right there at home. I would be foolish to make a change.'

'Sixty-four students.' Dave whistled. 'Isn't

167

that how many you have now? If every teacher in every town throughout the nation produced that many professional musicians, the world would be submerged in music.'

Sandy laughed as she continued to stare into the empty store window. 'Who said anything about producing professional musicians? It's possible that a few of my pupils may want to go into performing or teaching professionally, but they'll be in the minority. Most of my kids will never consider such a thing. I'll feel that I've succeeded if I just help a few of them to be functional musicians.'

'What do you consider the duties of a functional musician?' Dave asked.

'A functional musician fills a need in a community. It's a person who can perform at church or civic functions. It's a musician who can accompany a soloist, that sort of thing. I suppose many of my pupils will never even reach that degree of proficiency. Many will only play for their own enjoyment.'

'The same as my art students will paint for their own enjoyment,' Dave said. 'That's important, too, Sandy. It's good to have a worthwhile hobby that takes one's mind from everyday chores. But some of my students won't be able to do even that. Some just have no knack for painting or sketching. They simply can't master the rudiments.'

'But they'll always remember their art lessons,' Sandy said. 'And that, too, is important. Ten years from now some of my pupils won't be able to play a simple melody, but they'll have an understanding and an appreciation of music performed by others. They'll respect accomplished musicians. I don't believe that any learning is ever wasted.'

The warm May days marched relentlessly toward June, and Sandy filled the emptiness in her life with projects that required her to work harder. The morning-coffee recital she planned for her adult students was a success. Two of her advanced high-school pupils had a joint recital that was well received by the community. And her first-year beginners enjoyed more musical evening parties. Sandy tried to fill every free moment with some worthwhile activity.

One day toward the end of May Sandy made an appointment with Dr. Ward, which she kept a secret from Aunt Lotia. Her aunt had seemed strangely withdrawn and distant the past few weeks, and as she never mentioned her planned surgery, Sandy began to worry. When she brought up the subject, her aunt directed the conversation into other channels. At last Sandy decided it was time to take some action of her own.

Perhaps her aunt secretly feared the surgery because of her heart condition. It would be like her to keep her doubts and fears to herself.

Dr. Ward's waiting room reeked of

medicinal odors, but Sandy didn't mind. In fact, she hardly noticed them. She was intent on the questions she wanted to ask the doctor. She barely heard the background music flowing into the room until the receptionist raised her voice above it to call Sandy's name.

'Miss Stafford. Miss Sandy Stafford. The doctor will see you now. Follow me, please.'

Sandy followed the nurse into a small examining room, and the nurse closed the door behind them.

'What did you want to see the doctor about?' The nurse motioned Sandy to a chair as she prepared the examining table and shook a thermometer.

'I'm not sick,' Sandy assured her. 'I just want to talk to Dr. Ward about my aunt, Lotia Stafford. I need to speak to him privately, and I thought it was best just to make an appointment.'

'Make yourself comfortable.' The nurse put the thermometer away. 'Dr. Ward will be in in just a few moments.'

Sandy waited for several minutes. She read the medical certificates and diplomas framed in black against the cream-colored walls. She was beginning to read the labels on medicine bottles when Dr. Ward stepped into the room. He was a tall man with slightly stooped shoulders and steel-gray hair, and he smelled faintly of pipe tobacco. His blue eyes were bright and kindly, and Sandy met their direct gaze.

'I've come to talk to you about Aunt Lotia, Dr. Ward. She told me that she wanted to have some cosmetic surgery on those scars on her chin and neck, but she hasn't spoken of it for some time now. I've been worried.'

'There's no reason why she shouldn't have the surgery any time she wants it,' Dr. Ward replied. 'I've discussed it with her several times, and we're waiting now to hear from the specialist who will perform the operation.'

Sandy squirmed. 'Dr. Ward, is it safe for Aunt Lotia to go through with this? Really safe?'

'I see no reason why not.' Dr. Ward's gaze was steady. 'Of course, there's always an element of risk in any surgery. But your aunt is in excellent health for a woman her age.'

'But what about her heart?' Sandy blurted the question. 'That's what has me so concerned. I thought it was dangerous for people with heart trouble to undergo surgery. Am I mistaken?'

'Heart trouble?' Dr. Ward filled his pipe, and there was a long pause as he lighted it. 'Your aunt's heart is sound, always has been. There's nothing to worry about there. She's never had a history of any sort of heart disorder. I've treated her for years, and I give you my word. I know you're concerned about your aunt, Sandy, but you just relax. She's healthy, and she'll be in good hands. Getting

171

rid of those scars will give her a psychological lift that may add years of enjoyment to her life.'

Sandy felt numb. Somehow she managed to thank the doctor and walk from his office without making a fool of herself. But when Dave accidentally met her on the street a few minutes later, she was still in a daze.

'Sandy!' Dave was almost shouting. 'I spoke to you three times. Are you snubbing me? What have I done? What's the matter?'

'It's Aunt Lotia.' Sandy stared at Dave without really seeing him, and she repeated, 'It's Aunt Lotia.'

'She's sick? She can't be. I saw her only a few minutes ago. I've just come from the house and—'

'No, she's not sick. At least that's what Dr. Ward just told me.' Sandy looked at Dave appealingly. 'Doctors don't lie to their patients, do they? They wouldn't dare. Aunt Lotia must be the one who isn't telling the truth. I can hardly believe it.'

'You're not making sense.' Dave stared at Sandy through lowered eyelids.

'Don't you remember? The reason I'm here in Brunston right this minute is because I thought Aunt Lotia had a heart condition. I gave up . . . everything because I thought she needed me. Yet Dr. Ward just told me that her heart is sound. He says she's never had any problems with her heart. He says she's perfectly healthy for a woman of her age.'

'Maybe you'd better check with her,' Dave said. 'There seems to be a mix-up somewhere. I have the car parked down the street. Let me take you home. You look as if you might not make it on foot.'

Sandy was grateful for the ride. What would she do without Dave? He was right. She was not sure that her legs would have carried her the few blocks to her aunt's house.

Once Sandy was in the living room, she didn't know what to say. She wished that Dave had come inside with her. His presence would have given her courage and strength.

Aunt Lotia sat in her favorite rocker reading. The fragrance of vegetable soup drifted in from the kitchen. For a moment Sandy felt as if she might be losing her sanity.

'Sandy, you look pale.' Aunt Lotia studied her niece's face for a long moment. 'You're simply going to have to cut down on your work load. You need rest.'

Sandy ignored her aunt's words. If she was pale, it was not a result of overworking. She approached her subject head on.

'Aunt Lotia, I've just come from an appointment with Dr. Ward. He tells me that you have no heart condition, that you never have had any sort of heart trouble. Do you have an explanation?'

'Dr. Ward's absolutely right,' Aunt Lotia said in a low voice. She pressed her lips into a thin white line. 'I lied to you, Sandy. I lied to you because it was important to me to keep you here in Brunston.'

Sandy dropped onto the sofa, feeling as if her knees might buckle beneath her. 'But why? Why?'

'Because I've always been poor, that's why.' Aunt Lotia spat the words, and her eyes flashed. 'I've always had to scrimp and save and make do. This house is elegant, but no one knows what goes on behind its walls and windows except me. I've had to sew my own clothes, raise my own vegetables, shop at second-hand stores. Do you really think I enjoyed all that? Oh, I put up a good front. I spoke of original designer fashions and the superb flavor of home-grown produce. I never mentioned the drudgery behind it all. That was my big secret.'

Aunt Lotia continued her tirade like some mechanical toy that had been overwound.

'I wanted something better for you, Sandy, and when Bart Towner came back to Brunston, I decided that he was it. I had always liked him. He was what I wanted for you. If you hadn't been so stubborn, so idealistic, you could have been Mrs. Barton Towner. You would never have had another financial worry.'

Sandy rose from the sofa. Moments before she had been overcome by weakness, but now she felt as if great waves of energy were whirling inside her, propelling her into action.

Dashing upstairs, she threw clothing and toilet articles into a suitcase and banged it shut. With it in one hand and her coat over her arm, she raced back down the stairs, only to have her aunt block her path in the narrow hallway.

'Sandy, stop! Sandy, where are you going? Don't rush off this way!' Aunt Lotia's face was flushed, and she wrung her hands. 'Sandy! Be reasonable! You know how much this means to me now. Perhaps it isn't too late. You could sit on your pride. You could apologize to Bart. You could—'

Sandy elbowed past her aunt. 'Don't try to stop me, Aunt Lotia. I'll never spend another night in this house as long as I live. Never!'

CHAPTER FIFTEEN

Sandy spent her first night away from home at the Brunston Hotel, but the next day she moved into a less expensive rooming house. She hardly noticed its drabness. As seen through her anger, the whole world seemed to be wrapped in a glaring red haze.

Somehow Sandy managed to control her emotions long enough to cancel all her lessons. While she was at it, she canceled all plans for summer activities, then she sat alone in an angry, brooding silence. How could Aunt Lotia have done this to her? How could she!

Although the landlady summoned her to the telephone at frequent intervals, Sandy refused all calls. She certainly didn't want to talk to her aunt, nor to anyone else.

It was only when a knock sounded on her door and Dave's calm voice penetrated the thick panel that she faced the outer world. She opened the door and was greeted by the faint odor of turpentine.

'Sandy!' That one word, along with the expression on Dave's face, snapped Sandy to attention.

'I've called and called. Why haven't you answered? Couldn't you guess that I'd be worried about you?'

'I couldn't think of anyone that I wanted to talk to.' Sandy stepped back so that Dave could enter. 'Not one soul.'

'Not even me.' It was a statement, not a question, and the flatness of Dave's voice was like a slap.

'I didn't think about your calling. I'm sorry, Dave. I just thought about Aunt Lotia. And I have nothing more to say to her. Nothing at all. I'm leaving Brunston, you know. I'm going just as soon as I can make the arrangements.' She motioned Dave to a chair, but, as was his preference, he sat down on the floor.

'Do I get any sort of an explanation?' Dave asked. 'I know you must have had a bitter argument with your aunt. And I suppose it's none of my business, but during all this time I've come to consider you a friend, Sandy. A close friend. I know I live like a peasant and that we're worlds apart, but were you going away without ever saying good-bye?'

For the first time since she left home, Sandy saw herself as Dave must be seeing her. How presumptuous she had been to assume that he knew all about her troubles just because they were such a big thing in her own life.

Then words poured out of her in torrents. And somehow telling Dave about the terrible trick her aunt had played on her made her feel better. The pent-up explosive feeling diminished to a dull ache.

'She was so deceitful, Dave. I still can't believe it. She said she didn't want her relatives to know about her condition because it would worry them. Hah! She didn't want them to know because she knew they might see through her life. How could I have been so gullible, so stupid!'

'You're neither gullible nor stupid. And I don't blame you for being angry, but—'

'She used you too, Dave.' Sandy flopped down on an upholstered couch, and dust flew up into her face. 'You were a part of her scheme. She told me that I could only teach until seven each evening because you objected to late-evening disturbances, the coming and going of pupils. How about that! She was

177

attributing her desires to you. She was the one who objected to late-evening lessons. If I had kept a late schedule, then I wouldn't have been able to go out on dates with Bart. I should have been smart enough to have figured that out.'

'I can respect your righteous anger,' Dave said. 'Everyone's experienced a situation in which he's been wronged. But you can't let this incident ruin your life. You can't give it that much importance.'

'Let it ruin my life!' Sandy exclaimed. 'It *has* ruined my life! I had plans, important plans. And I had no defense. Aunt Lotia had never lied to me before. Never. I had every reason to trust her, to do my best for her.'

'Her lie may have ruined a year of your life,' Dave admitted, 'but if you keep carrying on like this, it will be your own bitterness that'll ruin the rest of it. You're going to have to get a hold on yourself. Remember, nobody promised you fairness, not even from your Aunt Lotia.'

'Did you come here to make me feel better or worse?' Sandy demanded. 'I thought you were my friend, Dave.'

'I am,' Dave assured her. 'And what I really came here for, besides finding out if you were okay, was to tell you that your aunt will undergo surgery day after tomorrow. She wanted you to know, but she couldn't get you on the telephone. The specialist had a sudden cancellation in his schedule, and he's going to work your aunt in sooner than she expected.'

Sandy stared at Dave without speaking.

'You're not going to back out on providing part of the funds, are you?' Dave said, frowning. 'No one would blame you if you did, but you aren't, are you?'

Sandy hesitated. 'It would serve Aunt Lotia right if I did. I'm sure that she wants that operation as much as I wanted to take that job in Chicago. I could get even with her, and it would serve her right.'

Dave turned to leave the room, but not before Sandy read the disappointment in his eyes.

'Oh, Dave! I can't be that vindictive. You know I'll keep my end of the bargain no matter what. I really will. I want Aunt Lotia to have the surgery. But just as soon as I can make arrangements, I'm moving to Chicago. I'll find work there somewhere. I could even start a private piano studio; I've had lots of that experience. Anyway, I'm leaving Brunston, and I'll never speak or think of this town again.'

During the next two days Sandy kept in touch with Dr. Ward. Although she didn't have to, she made a down-payment on the surgeon's fee and turned in the insurance policy numbers to the Des Moines hospital where the operation would take place. But it was only Dave's insistence, a day after surgery, that made her visit her aunt in the hospital.

179

'I'm going to drive to Des Moines to see her this evening, and you'd better come along,' Dave said as Sandy admitted him to her rented quarters. 'This is no time to let an argument come between you. Some sort of complications have set in. Two of your aunt's sisters are taking turns staying with her at the hospital.'

'They probably think I'm the world's Number One heel,' Sandy said. 'And I really can't tell them any differently. If Aunt Lotia wants them to know about our difficulties, she can be the one to tell them.'

'She can't tell them anything,' Dave said. 'Not a word. She's under heavy sedation—has been for the last twenty-four hours. At least that's the report from Dr. Ward. I called to check.'

Sandy got her purse and sweater. 'Let's go. I'll try to be pleasant when we get there, and I do appreciate your trying to help me, Dave. Forgive me for not being more cooperative.'

The drive to Des Moines seemed endless. The two-lane highway was narrow and hilly and beset with traffic. But Dave didn't seem to mind. He didn't get tense, and Sandy knew that he was studying the colors in the passing scenery.

When they finally reached downtown Des Moines, it took Dave a long time to find the hospital. The parking lot was full, and it took longer to park the car. Although Sandy was reluctant to make an appearance before her aunts, something inside her urged her to hurry.

She and Dave finally reached the hospital, and once they were inside the building, she was all but overcome by the medicinal odors in the air. The receptionist at the desk informed them where Aunt Lotia's room was, but when they approached it, the floor nurse on duty stopped them.

'Miss Stafford may have no visitors,' she said. 'Some of the family are waiting in the relatives' lounge down the hall. You may wait there if you care to.'

'That's too bad,' Sandy whispered to Dave. 'And after you've driven all this way. Do you suppose it means that she's taken a turn for the worse?'

'I have no idea what it means,' Dave said. 'But as for myself, I don't mind at all. I really came here to bring you along. I respect and admire your aunt and I wish her the best, but you're the one who belongs with her, you know. You really do.'

'You make me feel small and mean, Dave.'

Sandy dreaded going into the lounge to wait. But she forced herself to do it. What would her aunts think of her? Once inside, she greeted Aunt Addie and Aunt Cecile with kisses and hugs.

'Thank goodness you're here,' Aunt Cecile said, holding a perfumed handkerchief to her nose. 'We've thought all along that Lotia might rally if she knew you were here with her.'

181

'I'm going to call Dr. Meecher immediately,' Aunt Addie said. 'I'll see that you get in to see her tonight in spite of the no-visitors order.'

'You won't need to call him,' Aunt Cecile said. 'He's coming down the corridor right now. I caught sight of him through the doorway.'

Sandy felt very small as her aunts introduced her to the famous surgeon. What must Dr. Meecher think of her!

Drawing Sandy aside, Dr. Meecher, a short, heavy man, spoke softly to her. 'I understand from the family that there's been a rift between you and your aunt. She even tried to tell me a bit about it, but speaking of it upset her. Are you sure you want to see her?'

'I want to do what is best for her,' Sandy said. 'I've come here from Brunston. Aunt Lotia and I have had a serious difference of opinion, but if there is any way in which I can help her, I want to do it.'

'I felt sure that you would,' Dr. Meecher replied. 'You may go into her room now. Take her hand. Speak to her. She may or may not respond, but that's all you can do at this time. She is very weak and still under medication.'

There was nothing for Sandy to do but enter Aunt Lotia's room. Involuntarily she gasped as she saw her aunt's head swathed in bandages and her form quiet and still under the white sheet on the high hospital bed. For all her height and bulk, Aunt Lotia now seemed very

182

small and vulnerable.

Sandy stepped closer to the bed. She could hear her aunt's shallow breathing and caught the scent of body lotion that the nurses must have used in ministering to her. Slowly Sandy reached for her aunt's hand. It felt warm between her own icy fingers, and tears stung her eyelids.

'Aunt Lotia.' Sandy spoke the words softly, wondering if her aunt could hear through all the bandages. When she received no reply, she repeated her words a bit louder. 'Aunt Lotia, it's me, Sandy. Can you hear me, Aunt Lotia?'

CHAPTER SIXTEEN

As Sandy leaned over the hospital bed, her aunt's eyes fluttered open. For a moment she stared at Sandy blankly, then she seemed to recognize her niece, and a weak smile played on her lips. She squeezed Sandy's hand, but her voice was barely a whisper when she spoke.

'Forgive me, Sandy? Tell me that you forgive me?'

Sandy hesitated. Was this a death-bed request? Should she be making a death-bed promise? Before she had to answer, Dr. Meecher stepped into the room.

'Time's up, Sandy. You may come in again first thing in the morning, but I must ask you to leave now.'

Sandy laid her aunt's hand gently back on the bed and covered it with the sheet before she hurried to the doctor's side.

'Please, I need a few more minutes with her right now. You know about our quarrel. This is the first time I've seen my aunt since then. She spoke to me just now. I'm sure she recognized me. She asked me to—to forgive her. Please, may I stay with her a few more minutes?'

'Are you ready to forgive her?' Dr. Meecher asked, his steady gaze probing Sandy's face.

'I'm not sure,' Sandy whispered.

'Before you make your decision, I'd like to talk with you privately for a few minutes. You may see your aunt again in the morning. Right now come with me for a few words.'

Dr. Meecher led Sandy down the deserted hospital corridor to a small consulting room. He motioned her to a chair and closed the door behind them.

'Your aunt told me all about your quarrel. I can understand your feelings. Of course she was in the wrong. Of course you're angry and upset. Who wouldn't be? But you must forgive her, Sandy. You have no alternative, you know.'

'Forgive and forget.' Sandy gave a bitter laugh. 'Turn the other cheek. I've heard all that advice before, but I'm not sure I can manage to carry it out. I'm not that good a person, Dr. Meecher. I'm planning to leave

Brunston, to move to Chicago, to pick up the pieces of my life and put them together in the pattern I had planned before I was graduated from college.'

'That won't work,' Dr. Meecher said. 'It really won't. You're mistaken if you think you need to forgive your aunt in order for you to be good. Your personal virtue and goodness have nothing to do with this situation. You need to forgive your aunt in order to be happy. It's as simple as that.'

'In order to be happy?' Sandy studied the doctor's face to see if he was joking. But his expression was calm and serious.

'You're carrying a grudge, Sandy. And a grudge is an emotional scar. It's just as disfiguring as the scars that used to be on your aunt's face. The only way to remove a grudge is to cut it out of your life with the knife of forgiveness. Think about that before you go in to see your aunt again.'

With a smile, he dismissed her, and she tiptoed past the room where her relatives kept vigil. She hurried down the stairs and out the hospital door to escape into the coolness of the starlit night.

Sitting down on the hospital steps, she leaned against a concrete pillar and stared at the sky. Chagrined, she thought of the advice she had given Bart about forgiving himself. Could *she* forgive? Could she take her own advice? Or was she only adept at dishing it

185

out?

Sandy didn't know how long she sat there reliving the past before Dave's voice broke into her thoughts.

'So here you are! I've been looking everywhere for you. I thought you'd be upstairs with your aunts. And when you weren't . . .'

'Dave! How thoughtless of me!' Sandy jumped up. 'You must have wanted to go home hours ago. I've no idea what time it is.'

'I'm in no hurry to go. We'll leave when you're sure you're ready.'

'I think I'll stay here all night,' Sandy said slowly. 'It's so late now.' She glanced at her watch. 'It's almost midnight. And I want to talk to Aunt Lotia again first thing in the morning. You go ahead and go home. I can take a bus to Brunston sometime tomorrow.'

'I'll stay here with you,' Dave said. 'There are couches in that waiting room where we can catch a catnap, or you could sleep in the car if you want to.' Dave sat down on the steps.

'Guess I'll stay awake,' Sandy said. 'I can't sleep; I need to think.'

She and Dave sat in silence for a long time. Cars swished past the hospital. Crickets chirped on the open expanse of lawn. Moths fluttered to the bright lights on either side of the hospital door.

'What's your secret, Dave?' Sandy asked at last. 'How do you keep from hating your father

186

for being a drunk, for not supporting his family, for shoving his responsibilities onto you? How do you stay so even-tempered?'

'I did hate Dad for a long time,' Dave admitted. 'And I was miserable. I condemned him for his drinking.'

'I don't blame you,' Sandy said. 'Yours was another case of rightful anger. How could you feel otherwise! Yet you've changed. You're kind to him. You don't seek revenge. I sense a great strength in your gentleness toward him and toward the rest of your family. I wish some of it would rub off on me.'

'I think I forgave Dad on the day that I realized I was enjoying my sense of condemnation. It made me feel superior. And everyone likes to feel superior. But that was the wrong kind of superiority. And I knew it. It shamed me into developing my artistic talent. It shamed me into knowing that Dad was sick and that it was no challenge to be superior to a sick man.'

'Dave, leave me alone now,' Sandy said gently. 'Don't be hurt, but try to understand that I need to be alone to figure all this out for myself. You have helped me. I think I'm on the right track at last.'

The night grew damp and chilly, but Sandy hardly noticed as she tied a chiffon scarf around her hair and buttoned her sweater. She remembered how Dave had wanted to be able to understand good music, how he wanted to listen to it from her point of view. And when he accomplished this, a new world of music had opened up for him.

For the first time Sandy thought of her aunt's actions from her aunt's point of view. Aunt Lotia had always been poor. Her life had had dignity and value, but always in the background was the constant and nagging worry about money. It was only natural that Aunt Lotia should want better things for her niece. And to Aunt Lotia the better things, the freedom from financial worry and the social position that money could buy, were wrapped up in a brilliant package named Bart Towner. It was as simple as that.

Sandy watched the sun rise and later seemed to feel the reflection of the pinks and golds within herself as she hurried into the hospital and up the stairs to her aunt's floor.

Nurses on the day shift were beginning their morning duties. Aunt Addie and Aunt Cecile were still dozing in the waiting room, and Sandy didn't awaken them.

The head nurse approached Sandy, checking notes on her clipboard.

'Miss Sandy Stafford?'

Sandy nodded.

'Dr. Meecher left word that you may be admitted to your aunt's room at whatever time you arrive. You may stay for ten minutes.'

Smiling, Sandy thanked the nurse and then tiptoed into her aunt's dimly lighted room. To her surprise, she saw that her aunt's eyes were open and that she was trying to smile through all the bandages.

'Sandy.' Aunt Lotia's voice was muffled and weak. 'You've come back to me. I was afraid that you were gone for good. Couldn't blame you if you were.'

'I've been here at the hospital all night,' Sandy told her. 'But I've come to you now to tell you that there's nothing for me to forgive. You made a mistake, but the mistake does not make *you*. *You're* still my Aunt Lotia, and we need each other as much as ever.'

Aunt Lotia smiled and closed her eyes without speaking, but Sandy knew that she had understood her. When she tiptoed from the room, she faced her other aunts and could honestly tell them that Aunt Lotia was better, a fact that Dr. Meecher verified when he stopped by on his morning rounds.

Leaving the hospital, Sandy hurried out to the parking lot where Dave had moved his car. She opened the door and smiled into his sleep-fogged face.

'Dave! If we pool our money we can rent that empty store building for a studio—a combination art and music studio. We can paint the walls, hang a few draperies, move in some easels and a piano. How about it?'

Dave grinned. 'Thought you were going to Chicago.'

'Plans have changed. What's Chicago got

that I need? Nothing. Do you realize what I've done in Brunston? I've built myself a career— a life. Of course, I'll have to keep on building or it will die, but I'm a lot more independent in Brunston teaching privately than I would ever be in the Chicago school system.'

Dave leaned over and gave Sandy a kiss. He asked no questions, and they made no more plans, but Sandy knew, without any words being spoken, that they had an understanding. And she knew that Aunt Lotia would approve.

We hope you have enjoyed this Large Print book. Other Chivers Press or Thorndike Press Large Print books are available at your library or directly from the publishers.

For more information about current and forthcoming titles, please call or write, without obligation, to:

Chivers Large Print
published by BBC Audiobooks Ltd
St James House, The Square
Lower Bristol Road
Bath BA2 3BH
UK
email: bbcaudiobooks@bbc.co.uk
www.bbcaudiobooks.co.uk

OR

Thorndike Press
295 Kennedy Memorial Drive
Waterville
Maine 04901
USA
www.gale.com/thorndike
www.gale.com/wheeler

All our Large Print titles are designed for easy reading, and all our books are made to last.